KING OF THE FAE

A PARANORMAL ROMANCE

AVA MASON

PROLOGUE

Everyone's twenty-first birthday is supposed to be something to remember. It's a milestone, a step into real adulthood. Mine was when everything changed. That's the day the men showed up. Everywhere I went, they watched me, creeping closer, trying to find a second when I was alone. They all wanted the same thing; to capture me and bring me back to their world.

One was different. Dark, mysterious, and sexy, he stood out from the rest.

He had come for my blood.

CHAPTER 1

Kip

"And here they entered The Mist Realms, home to beautiful, tiny creatures so delicate their touch is like a fine rain on your cheek. Walking through these surroundings was enough to almost make them forget the death just beyond the borders."

My eyes lifted from the pages of the antique book I'd been flipping through and locked on Mac.

"This story slipped into a dark place pretty quickly," I told him.

The old man laughed, his pale blue eyes sparkling as he brushed his trusty dusting cloth over a book that hadn't seen the light of day in years and tucked it back on the shelf in front of him.

"Not quickly," he corrected me. "It's been building up."

He winked as he moved on to the next book from the stack that climbed tenuously from the dark-carpeted floor to his waist level where he teetered atop an ancient stepstool. This was his favorite activity for the long stretches of empty days when business at the bookshop ran slow. He started in the back corner next to one of the many shelves, cases, or stacks, climbed atop his stool, and dusted every book until he made it to the front corner.

I knew one of these days he was going to get too cocky with his leaning ability and end up toppling headfirst into a mound of retro pulp thrillers. That would put an interesting spin on the story he'd been telling me since I first started working there. It wasn't every time I worked. Instead, the intricate story came in spurts. Mac gave me little details of his sprawling imagined world whenever they seemed to form in his head. Sometimes he'd see something in one of the books or hear a comment and add another bit like an anecdote he just had to share.

It was one of the most unique parts of the eccentric man. I adored it as much as I adored the rest of him. At least he kept me entertained when it seemed that the people of Glendale had reached their reading quota. We hadn't seen a customer in a week. Which brought us to that day, the lingering tail of both a heat wave and a business dry spell.

A gust of hot air swooped into the shop as the front door opened and Mac and I both looked up expectantly. Maybe someone needed a book to read while they sipped lemonade in a hammock or floated around on a pool raft. Maybe they'd embarked on a courageous journey through the town and needed to seek refuge in the cool air conditioning of the shop. Either way, we'd take it.

"Oh," Mac said when he saw Harley crossing toward me.

Her grin dropped as he reached for the next book in the stack and I went back to flipping through the book on the counter in front of me.

"Hey, Harley," I said.

"Don't seem so thrilled to see me," she frowned, her deep blue eyes clouded as she flung her raven black hair behind her.

"I'm sorry," I said. "We just haven't had a customer in... at this point it seems like ever. We thought you might be one."

This seemed to mollify my best friend, who made her way over to the counter. She used two fingers to lift the corner of my book cover and glance at the title.

"Riveting," she said, dropping it back down. "I know business is just rocking here today, but maybe you can slip out a little early."

"I still have another hour of my shift," I told her.

"Mac, you can handle the rest of the day on your own so Kip here can get a jump on celebrating her birthday, right?" she called toward the tower of books. Mac's hand appeared around the edge of the bookshelf, flashing her a thumbs-up. "See? He's got this."

"I can't just leave him," I told her. "It's just one more hour."

"He's *fine*," Harley argued, tugging on my arm to guide me around the counter. "We can get a whole extra hour of partying in. You only turn twenty-one once. Come on."

"Fine, but let's keep it to a level where I'm going to get to turn twenty-two."

There was no point in arguing. Harley's head was already at the bar and probably four drinks in. She was far more excited about heading out for the night than I was. Truth be told, if I'd planned my birthday it probably would have involved a pizza and bad movie in my favorite pajamas. But Harley had big things in mind and none of them involved fuzzy slippers. It was status quo for our friendship. Our opposing appearances and personalities meant we didn't seem like we would be as close as we were. Spending our early childhood together in the foster system had overcome that and cemented our bond. Now we just navigated those differences whenever they came up.

Like the night of my twenty-first birthday.

Harley brought me home and waited impatiently as I went through several outfits. None of them were as comfortable as the pajamas folded on the foot of my bed, but we finally settled on my birthday look and headed out. By the time we got to the bar some of Harley's enthusiasm rubbed off on me and I was ready to have fun. Harley was much more of a drinker than I was, even on this particular birthday, but watching her having a good time was a party in and of itself.

Watching Harley do just about anything was an experience. From the tattoos that lined her arms to her withering black-rimmed eyes and a wardrobe dark enough to mourn whole populations, she stood out. Her personality matched, which meant everywhere we went, we were bound to be the center of attention.

That was definitely the case when she took back a flaming shot, toasted me, then chased it with a beer, to the enthralled cheers of the people around us.

"You are lagging behind, Kip," Harley said, nudging a vibrant green Jell-O shot toward me.

"Still working on this guy," I told her, indicating the beer I'd been sipping all night. I leaned toward her. "Speaking of guys, did you notice that one?"

I swept my eyes to the side and tilted my head, trying to subtly indicate the man I'd noticed watching us since we first got there. Harley was about three drinks past being able to follow me, so I leaned again and pointed.

"Who?" she asked.

"Right over there by the bar," I whispered. "Wearing a suit."

"A *suit*?" she asked incredulously. "Kip, this bar has not seen a suit since the day it was bought."

"He is right at the corner of the bar. I think he's watching us."

She moved her head back and forth like she was looking through the people stuffed onto the small dance floor.

"That's a woman," Harley said.

"He has long hair," I told her.

"Nope, it's a woman."

"It is not a..." I threw subtlety to the wind and turned around. "That's a woman."

"Told you," Harley said.

Confusion settled in. I knew there'd been a man standing at the corner of the bar watching us. Turning back to her, I started to question the strength of the drink she'd bought me when a loud shout and a crash stopped me. Someone hit my legs from behind and I tumbled backward. Harley yelled my name and reached for me, but her hand slipped away. The impact of my back hitting the ground knocked the wind out of me, and before I could get myself under control, something hard hit me in the side. I tumbled across the carpet and right into the middle of a brawl.

I could hear Harley shouting and men's grunts that probably followed her elbowing them to get out of the way. Getting to my knees, I tried to stand, but a stumbling man lunged toward someone behind me, making me fall back again. Suddenly strong hands grabbed me and yanked me up off the floor. My mind was spinning, making everything swirl around me. I barely realized that the ground was solid beneath my feet again when whoever rescued me set me down near the door. His hands pressed down on my shoulders until I was steady and I looked up at him.

My eyes caught his and I felt a shiver run through me. His hair was long and thick, pooling over one shoulder, but there wasn't a single thing feminine about this man. He was tall, so tall my neck hurt to look at him. With wide, muscular shoulders and a broad chest that filled his finely tailored suit. His body was so close to mine, I could feel the heat radiating off it, and my heart pounded wildly in my chest. A look suddenly flashed in his eyes and he growled low in his throat as he grabbed my shoulders and pushed me aside again. I was about to lash out at him when I noticed part of a broken chair land just where I'd been standing.

"Thank you," I said, stumbling over the words.

"No problem." The man smirked and I felt tiny under the

combined effect of his intense masculinity. The way he stared at me like I was small and insignificant. So much so, that he knew he had to protect me. Without another word, he turned and faded into the crowd.

"Kip! Are you okay?" Harley demanded, forcing her way through the crowd to me.

"That was him," I told her, pointing after the man who'd pulled me out of the fight. "The man who was standing at the bar."

"I thought we established that was a woman," Harley said.

I shook my head.

"No, it was him," I insisted.

"Come on," she said, looping her arm around my shoulders. "Let's go. I think we've had enough for the night."

She led me out of the bar and my eyes swept along the sidewalk, trying to find the man, but he was gone.

Mac had made enough progress on his stack of books by the time I got into work the next morning that he'd pushed the stepstool aside.

"Did you have a good birthday?" he asked.

I would have answered him, but too much of my concentration was on the men scattered throughout the shop. Five of them milled around, roaming in and out of the aisles and running their fingertips along the spines of random books in that distinct way that said they weren't paying any attention to the titles. As soon as I took a few steps into the shop, their eyes all moved to me. I stopped in my tracks and they all smiled at me. It felt like I was stuck in one of those dreams where I came to work in nothing but my underwear. Last week that dream featured My Little Pony panties and a training bra. Not my finest nocturnal moment.

But this wasn't a dream. These men really were following my every move as I made my way behind the counter and clocked in for my shift.

"We have... customers." I couldn't help but betray the surprise in my voice.

"Mmm," Mac replied, not at all the reaction I was expecting. Instead of delight to have so many new faces in the shop, he watched them carefully, without the curiosity he usually had with customers. Instead, he seemed almost suspicious. He paid attention to every move they made and often shifted so he could keep track of them all. "I'll be here, if you need something." He pointed in a random direction and walked off.

One started toward me and promptly walked into the low table in front of him. Not missing a step, he snatched a book from the nearly toppling table and carried it over to me. As he got closer, something struck me about him. I couldn't put my finger on it, but something about the way he looked seemed off. I was still trying to figure it out when he sidled up to the counter and set the book down.

"Can I help you?" I gave him a smile.

"You might," he said. "I'm looking for a recommendation. Have you read this one?"

My eyes dropped to the glossy dust jacket on the hardcover book and then lifted back to him.

"I'm sorry, I haven't had much reason to read about the finer points of using my primal masculinity to snag women," I told him.

Making a quick mental note to discuss Mac's stocking choices with him, I eased the book back across the counter toward the man. Without anything else to say to me, he took it and loped off, dropping it back to the table where he'd gotten it.

Within seconds of him leaving, a blond man appeared. He clutched another book in his hands and grinned at me with unnerving intensity.

"You look like someone who knows her books," he said in a measured, almost eerily smooth tone.

"I do work in a bookshop," I pointed out. "Books are kind of my bag."

He burst into laughter, making me take a step back from him.

"Miss?" another of the men called from the shelves.

I fought the urge to roll my eyes. He'd caught my attention as soon as he walked in, but only because of the strange long jacket he wore.

"Yes?" I asked.

"Can you come over here and help me for a moment?"

I started toward him and the green-eyed man at the counter took a defensive step forward.

"She was helping me," he snapped.

"Mac, do you think you could help me out here?" I asked, looking over to the shelves where he was arranging a set of antique dictionaries.

"Oh, no, that's all right," Long Jacket said. "I'll wait for you."

As I was walking toward Blondie, I realized the one in the long jacket had the same strangeness about him as the first. It was like in the first instant I looked at them, they were impossibly attractive, but then something flickered and in that flicker, they changed. I couldn't quite describe it, but it was like seeing a different being, but only for an instant. It happened so fast, I couldn't really register it. Only after it happened did my mind catch up and notice the odd, split-second shift from normal, approachable men to some other creature.

Dear lord, what the hell did Harley put in my drink?

I got to the third man and realized he was standing in the romance section. The hair stood up on the back of my neck and I cringed as a slow smile crept across his face.

"Have you read any of these?" he asked in a slow drawl.

There was something seriously wrong here. Never in my life

had I attracted any particular sort of attention from men. My slight frame, head full of wild red curls, and sprinkle of freckles might get a side-eye every now and then, but these men seemed magnetized toward me.

I was not appreciating it nearly as much as someone might think. In fact, discomfort was building up through me and when the third man took a long stride toward me, closing my back against a full bookshelf, it seemed to surge up and out through my chest. In that same instant, several books from the top of the shelf slipped out of place and tumbled down on his head. It disoriented him enough that I had time to slip around him and back to the counter.

The books crashing down on the man left me rattled. It was almost like I'd willed it to happen when he came too close.

But that wasn't possible.

CHAPTER 2

Stryder

It wasn't supposed to be this hard.

I sat on the end of the bed in the tight hotel room, staring at my reflection in the large mirror. The eyes that stared back at me were cold and devoid of emotion, but beyond them was turmoil. I knew why I was here. There was only one thing that brought me to Glendale: kill the human who would destroy my people.

The woman I'd just saved.

The woman who made my heart pound, fire run through my veins and a protective instinct roar to life the minute she was in danger. The woman whom, also, I was tempted to entice into my bed, to learn every inch of her petite, sexy body, and never let her out of my sight.

Scowling, I squeezed closed my eyes as memories burst in my mind with searing brightness and clarity. I heard the clash of sword blades against each other and the cries of warriors before they hit the ground. The smell of rain on the dirt beneath my feet mixed with blood. On my back I could still feel the hot, slicing pain of the steel going through my skin.

It all reminded me of why I was there. The real reason, not the one that wanted to distract me with her sparkling green eyes. Whenever the thought of questioning my mission flickered through my mind, those memories were there to bring me back into the stark reality. The battlefields I had left behind were far from quiet. It was my responsibility, my duty to bring this all to an end, and the only way I was going to do that was to kill the one who was destined to protect my enemy.

But my target was nothing like I expected. I had come here with the full intention of going through with what I had to do without hesitation and without difficulty.

As soon as I saw her, everything changed.

She didn't seem capable of being a part of the atrocities I've seen. She was so innocent and unassuming. Even the way she looked at the people around her made me question what I've been told. Those eyes didn't hold the darkness I'd expected. Except, she must have *something* within her to preserve the evil reign and push the bloody war on. Otherwise, I wouldn't be here.

My instructions were clear; I wasn't mistaken. She was the one I was sent to kill.

And yet, something about this woman drew me to her. I didn't know what it was and I couldn't explain it, but the instant I saw her, my focus on my mission disappeared. Standing there in the bar, all I wanted to do was watch her. It wasn't because I was trying to get close enough to her to find a way to kill her. Or even because I wanted to learn more about her to simplify my task. There was a compulsion inside me to watch her movements and monitor the people around her. I didn't like it when they got too close to her. The instant I saw she was in danger, an instinct to protect her overwhelmed me.

Remembering that feeling pushed me to my feet and I paced back and forth across the tight hotel room in frustration. I hadn't pushed back the curtains and the single wall sconce in between the two beds let out only meager light, making me feel like I was walking through shadows. That felt appropriate. Everything had been so clear, so unwavering when I left home to come here. Now I couldn't get the thoughts coursing through my head to make sense.

The brutal images flashed behind my eyes again. Bodies were scattered across the ground and faces far too young to experience any of it stared up at the sky like they were waiting for it all to have been a dream. But it wasn't. None of the horror we had experienced since the queen slashed and burned her way into power had been imagined. In fact, it had all been far worse than anything any of us could have created in our minds.

That's why I was here. It was why I had to do what I had to do. Either I killed this girl, or my people would be killed or turned into slaves. The horror of this reality pushed down on me, trying to drag me back, but I had to resist. I had to face this with courage and strength, knowing I was trading her life for countless others. The prophecy had been harsh, but straightforward and there was no way to escape it.

Even as I forced myself to think that, I could still feel the protective urge from the night before. This mission was only supposed to take a day. I should have been back in my own world by now. Yet, after walking into the bar with the full intention of luring her away to kill her, I did the opposite. My instinct had been to guard her, to save her from the violence that erupted around her, and I didn't know why. It didn't make sense and I was confused and angry.

There was something about her that was getting in my way and I needed to find out what it was.

Failure wasn't something I could even consider. There was

no way I could return and tell all those who were relying on me that I had let them down. It would be offering them to the slaughter. I had no choice left but to confront her. It would give me clarity of mind and put me back in focus.

Slipping into my jacket, I swept my hair back into a ponytail, secured in place by a leather band, and left the hotel. I'd been told to look for her at the bookshop in the small village and I headed directly there. If that wasn't where she was, I would have to track her, and I was hoping to avoid the inconvenience. The closer I got to the shop, the more confident I was that I'd found her. The same strange feeling from the night before drew me in, compelling me to pull the door open and step inside.

As soon as I did, my eyes locked on her. She was standing behind a counter, toward the center of the dimly lit, cluttered shop. Lords, she was beautiful. Hair the color of fire fell around her head in soft waves, framing stark cheekbones and a petite face. My chest buzzed at the sight of her.

She was leaning forward on the counter, flipping through the pages of one of the countless books filling every surface in the space. I couldn't tell what type of book it was, but she didn't seem engrossed in whatever was written. She looked up immediately when I approached her. Her eyes widened slightly, and I knew she remembered me from the bar. I'd faded into the crowd when I realized she had caught on to me watching her. There was no concealing myself when I picked her up from the ground and carried her away from the fight.

I decided then that would be the way I would reach out to her.

"It's good to see you up and about," I said. "How are you feeling today?"

She looked at me suspiciously, like she didn't want to go along with the conversation.

"Fine," she said. "But it's still early."

Her bright green eyes narrowed slightly, and I got the feeling she was testing me. It only took a few seconds for me to realize why. A man appeared from between two of the tightly positioned bookshelves and came toward her. My body tensed when he leaned against the counter.

"Now, I've been trying to get you in a conversation all day," he said. "Why don't you share some of that attention?"

"Because she's giving it to me." I gave him a stern look, wishing he would disappear.

The man looked at me and as soon as our eyes met, his expression faltered. He recognized me as much as I recognized the façade he was presenting to her. I wouldn't say anything. This wasn't the time or place to tell her the men crawling around her were anything more than human. My threatening glare was enough to push him back.

"Have a good day," the man muttered before slinking out of the shop.

"It seems you are quite the popular shopkeeper." I leaned down on the counter so that we were eye to eye. Her breath quickened and I could see her pulse hammer in her neck. I was tempted to lean closer and kiss her.

"More so lately." We locked eyes and I was unable to look away. Her eyes were a clear green, sparkling and so innocent. "But I'm actually not the shopkeeper. I'm the shop... helper. Mac owns the bookstore." She seemed flustered.

"What's your name?" My advisors hadn't told it to me when they sent me to her. They'd only described her and told me I would know her when I saw her.

They were right. I had known who she was the instant my eyes fell on her walking down the street toward the bar.

"Kip."

"Kip," I reached out, tracing the side of her hand, feeling a buzzing sensation in my finger. "Is Mac here?" I looked around.

"He stepped out to get some coffee." She leaned back, pulling her hand away from me and eyeing me suspiciously again. "He'll probably be back fairly soon if you want to meet him."

"No," I smiled. "I don't want to meet him. I was wondering if you could take a break. Maybe we could take a walk and get some fresh air that's a little less full of desperation."

A hint of a smile curved her lips, but she gestured toward the shop and the other men occasionally peering at her from around the displays of books. None of them were human. These were Fae men, but they weren't sent for the same mission as me. If they had been, I would know about them, yet I didn't recognize their faces. It meant they were from a different court, and that could only mean their presence had ominous reasons.

"Well, as you can see, I am just hopelessly busy." She gave me a coy smile, one meaning she wasn't sorry at all about that.

I was starting to answer when the door opened and she looked over my shoulder. Her face changed into recognition as the dark-haired woman from last night stalked up to the counter. She dropped a large black leather bag down onto it.

"Are you feeling better?" the girl asked. "Sore or anything?"

"Hello to you, too, Harley," the red-haired woman said, glancing at me.

"Are you feeling better after getting caught up in that mess last night?" Harley asked.

"I'm fine," Kip nodded. "I did exactly what you said and went right to bed."

"Sure you did." Even her friend could read her sarcasm.

I stepped away from the counter and Harley immediately shifted over to take my place. My impression of Harley was slight, if at all, as she continued to ramble at Kip. As Kip's eyes moved to me from Harley, the confusion inside me twisted harder. I didn't like that Harley was taking the attention off me. I wanted Kip's gaze to linger on me and only me.

Then, suddenly it did. Her eyes moved towards me again and my heart pounded. The illogical urge to swipe her off her feet, throw her over my shoulder and carry her away washed over me and I growled, frowning.

My mission just got ten times harder.

I needed to kill this woman, and be done with her. Or my people would die a gruesome, torturous death.

CHAPTER 3

Kip

"Are you seriously staring at that guy right behind me while I'm trying to talk to you?" Harley sounded pissed.

My eyes snapped back to her and I felt heat rush across my cheeks. I hated it when that happened. My parents could have at least passed down enough melanin so I didn't turn bright red anytime I was even slightly embarrassed. Not only did it make my cheeks look as bright as raspberries, but the freckles that were usually a pale scattering across the bridge of my nose popped out vibrantly against the blush. It wasn't exactly what I'd call sophisticated. Since I didn't have any memories of my natural parents, I couldn't even blame them. I assumed they'd looked pretty much like me, since my admittedly basic understanding of genetics told me I was a big old conglomeration of recessive genes. Until I had proof, I felt alone in my fluorescent flushing.

"I'm sorry," I told Harley. "You have to admit, he's kind of hard not to look at."

She flashed a glance over her shoulder and shrugged

noncommittally. "If you like that whole long hair, sleek suit, smoldering thing, I guess."

Truth be told, I had never really considered whether I liked that whole long hair, sleek suit, smoldering thing until it was standing in the classic literature section staring at me. But now that it was, I couldn't stop my eyes from wandering in his direction, wondering what he was doing here. Had he been asking me on a *date* before Harley interrupted us? If the man moved down two aisles into the mysteries section, it would be much more appropriate.

I felt immediately drawn to him, and at the same time was wary of the attraction. Not that I had spent my adult life anti-man or anything, but this pull was unlike anything I'd ever experienced. I couldn't help but acknowledge that his sudden appearance coincided with the other men who seemed to be coming out of the woodwork at me. He didn't strike me with the same immediate ick factor they did, but I was hesitant to let myself fall into it completely. He might have the same reason for latching on to me, just with more swagger.

"He's the one from the bar last night," I told her.

Harley sighed and dropped her head down in exasperation.

"Kip, we've gone over this. The person standing at the bar was a woman."

"It was when you looked over," I told her. "But that man was standing there. He also saved my ass when I got swept into that fight. You had to have seen him. He picked me up and carried me to the door."

"I didn't see shit. I was too worried about you and the man I'd just punched in the face. Mostly you."

"You punched someone?" I asked. Unfortunately, I wasn't surprised. It wasn't the first time Harley had lashed out like that.

"Did you forget that they knocked you over and you ended up curled up in the middle of the floor with them just wailing on each other all around you?" she asked.

"No, I distinctly remember that. It was one of the more unpleasant moments of my evening. But I also remember not being able to get myself together and him saving me."

Harley rolled her eyes. "All right, we're going to figure this out right now."

She looked over at the man and I reached across the counter to her. "Can we try to be at least a little bit subtle? This is where I work."

The words were barely out of my mouth before Harley made a sound that was probably her saying '*hey*,' but sounded almost like a bark. Subtlety was never her strongest suit. The man looked over at her, unaffected by her rough edges. That just impressed me more. Everybody was affected by Harley in one way or another.

"Yes?" His eyebrow twitched upwards, amused.

Harley gestured for him to come over and I gave him what I hoped was an apologetic look before she pounced. "Where were you last night?"

"You're just going to go right to it?" I whispered incredulously. "Without introduction or disclaimer?"

"I don't do trigger warnings," she hissed back at me, too loud for him not to notice.

"She knows where I was," the man said smoothly, nodding toward me. "Why don't you ask her?"

There was literally nothing about what he said that should have inspired another flush of color across my cheeks, yet there it was. This time accompanied by another sizzling across my chest. This attention was definitely different than what I was getting from the other men.

"I told you he was at the bar." I stared her down, a smug look on my face.

Harley looked back and forth between us. "So, you're telling me you really were standing there, watching us?"

"No," he said. "I wasn't watching you."

"See?" Harley gave me a satisfied look.

"I was watching her," he told her, snipping the end of her word.

"You were what?" Harley asked, obviously taken aback by his response.

I bit down into my bottom lip and looked away to keep myself from laughing. It wasn't every day I got to see usually unflustered and intensely confident Harley get thrown off her game. Even the situations that resulted in her decking somebody were fueled by anger or aggravation, not surprise.

"At the bar," his eyes wandered back to mine, intense and hypnotic. "I wasn't watching the two of you. Only her. And now, if she has a second, I'd like to get a recommendation for a book."

My eyes slid over to Harley, waiting for her reaction. She stared at him for another second, seeming to process what was happening, then the slightest smile twitched on her lips. "Go right ahead." She swept her hand dramatically, taking a step away from the counter.

I walked around the side of the counter and passed her to join him. She gave me a teasing nudge with her elbow as I passed, but I slapped at her hands, swatting her off. The man and I walked into the sea of books and I followed him on what felt like a random path through the shop until we got to a nook where Harley wouldn't be able to watch us.

"Is there something in particular you're looking for?" I was suddenly nervous.

"Yes." He smirked, his eyes tracing over my face appreciatively. "But since I'm here let's talk about books first."

"Cute," I said.

He gestured vaguely around us. "Tell me about some of these."

I glanced around, tapping my chin as if thinking deeply about the rows of crafting books. Most of them had come from a mass purge from one of the local housewives. She'd decided she wasn't cut out for transforming a year's worth of saved paper towel rolls into a heavily glittered Christmas decoration extravaganza.

"What are you into?" I asked. "Are you more of a needlework man? Or do you land more on the stamping and scrapbooking end of the spectrum?"

"Excuse me?"

"This is the section you chose." I indicated the books. "I just assumed you were interested in filling your free time with a new hobby."

He looked at the books like it was the first time he was noticing their titles. "Ahem," he said, shaking his head. "Um, probably none of them."

"Don't get discouraged," I kept my face straight. "Learning a new skill can be intimidating at first, but if you really put your mind to it and concentrate, you'll get it. I'm sure you could be quilting up a storm in no time."

He swiveled around, eyes narrowed as he took the books in. "Maybe I'll try my hand at needlework? I've always liked stabbing things." He grinned and it lit up his face.

I tried not to smile. "I really think you'd be good at it. In fact, if you hang around town for a bit longer, there's a convention at the end of every summer. I'm sure the ladies would be thrilled to have you join them."

"Very funny." He looked dismayed and I laughed.

"You have to make sure you bring a side dish, though. They are very serious about their potluck."

"So it seems I picked the wrong section. Though you shouldn't be so quick to judge. You never know," he said in a teasing tone, "maybe I sew with the best of them."

"Do you?" I asked.

He swallowed hard, his heated gaze meeting mine. "I could be convinced to try it, if you were to teach me." I froze, caught up like a deer in headlights as a warmth billowed in my stomach, spreading to my chest and arms, making my lips part. I exhaled a breath, unable to look away.

"Unfortunately, I don't know how." My heart pounded so loud, I hoped he couldn't hear it.

"No, of course." He shook his head, breaking the spell between us. "I mean, no," he said. "I just wanted to get you alone." My eyes widened in surprise and he hurried to finish his sentence. "For a walk. I wanted to revisit that idea of us taking a walk."

I didn't have a chance to answer him when the bells above the door jangled cheerfully to announce someone else coming in. I turned around, relieved for the interruption. Did I want to go on a walk with him? *Yes, please.* His utter sexy masculinity alone made heat prickle my skin.

But was it the safe thing to do? I wasn't so sure. Not with all the other weird stuff happening. "Oh, I need to see who this is."

I hustled back with him on my heels to a vantage point in the shop where I would be able to see. Mac grinned with a happy wave, then his eyes settled on the man behind me. His lips parted in surprise and I turned back towards the man. What was going on? The sexy man's eyes locked on the bookshop owner. His expression was suddenly tense, and his posture stiffened.

"I need to go," he said. "Think about it." Without waiting for me to answer him, he made his way quickly out of the shop, with Mac staring after him.

"I need to do some bookkeeping in the back." Mac hurried towards the back of the store, with me staring after him in wonder.

"What did he say to you?" Harley rushed up to me.

I blinked, then turned to look at Harley. "Nothing," I shrugged.

The expression on her face was unconvinced.

"Nothing? He dragged you off to some dark, isolated corner

and you're going to tell me he said nothing? Well," she added with a mischievous glint in her eye, "maybe he really did say nothing."

Sighing, I took my place back behind the counter. "He didn't drag me off anywhere. He walked with me at an appropriate customer-worker distance to a decently lit aisle of craft books."

"That's not nearly as fun," Harley said. "I'm going to tell people my story instead."

CHAPTER 4

Stryder

I slammed the hotel room door so hard it made the wall rattle and the piece of cheap generic artwork threaten to fall to the floor. Outside my door, 'Do Not Disturb' signs hanging from the door handles of rooms up and down the hallway, but I didn't care. Right then, it didn't matter to me who they were or what they were doing. I also didn't care if I disturbed the hell out of them. The frustration and anger inside me had reached a level that obliterated anything else my mind.

Going to the bookshop to see her was supposed to make this easier. It was supposed to clarify everything in my head. Show me I had just gotten too wrapped up in how unexpected she was. Then, I could finish what I'd come here to do and go home.

Instead, it only made things more confusing.

The images of the war closed in around me until it felt like they were crushing down, forcing me to acknowledge them. The Land of Sidhe was in torment, its realms torn apart by the vicious war that burned across the land with a fury none had been able to quell. Not that we had backed down. At every moment there were soldiers standing in the paths of the insurgents, cutting them off and hampering their progress as much as possible. My own warriors had been among the most courageous and many had pushed back valiantly for seemingly endless months without a break.

As much fervor and perseverance as my army showed, the enemies gave their own. They were deluded into their devotion to the queen, blinded by blood into believing in her power and not seeing her truth. The queen was the heartbeat of the brutality. Her threats against my court, along with the others, were getting more pressing by the day. It meant I didn't have much time to be here in the human world.

My kind needed me.

That, and only that, was why I had come to Glendale. The warlocks, my most trusted advisers, had sent me here, carrying within me the knowledge that the fate of the Land of Sidhe hinged on one singular woman.

Kip.

Even the name sounded innocent. Seeing her in the bookshop, away from the danger in the bar, was meant to put me back on track. The whole time I was there, I searched for something, *anything,* that would make what the warlocks told me about her make sense. They'd been so adamant. There wasn't a single shred of hesitation or uncertainty when they detailed the horrifying role Kip would play in the war raging through our world. Sending me here hadn't been an exploratory mission or a last-ditch effort to find out more about her. What they saw was clear and disquieting enough to direct me here with only one option in front of me.

Kill the human who threatened my whole world.

And yet, talking to her and hearing her laugh only made it harder.

I felt trapped in the hotel room, but there was nowhere else to go. Getting Kip alone in the shop had felt like an opportunity, but it was too risky with the others there. As long as she was in the bookshop, I couldn't even consider going after her. Her death wasn't meant to be a display or a call to action. Killing her wasn't sending a message. It was nothing more than a means to an end, and that's the only way it could play out. Drawing too much attention would only threaten my world further.

I couldn't stay in the room any longer. It was still early in the day and the thoughts were getting louder and more oppressive the faster they rushed through my head. There was no way I could stand them for the long hours alone in the room until the next day. Without any concept of where I might be going, I left the hotel room and walked out into the town again. Glendale was small, but surprisingly alive. People moved in and out of the rows of small shops on either side of the street and sections of the sidewalk were crowded as neighbors stopped to greet each other. I moved among them casually, giving off no indication that I didn't belong there.

Any of them looking at me would know no different. My glamour shielded them. They saw what they wanted to, a pleasing image that would silence any suspicion and lull them into trusting me. I could walk among them, taking up space in the town I had never visited, and no one would question it.

Movement out of the corner of my eye caught my attention. I looked across the street to see one of the men from the bookshop disappear into a store. Curiosity latched on to me and I let it guide me to the other sidewalk and through the frosted glass door. I needed to know why the other Fae were there. There had to be a very specific purpose. With so many of them there and none seeming to care about the others, I could only assume they knew about each other and shared the same goal.

That didn't reassure me; it only made me more suspicious. I heightened my awareness of my surroundings, trying to discover where the man had gone. The longer he stayed out of sight, the stronger my compulsion to find him became. I didn't like him or any of the others wandering the town without me knowing why they were here or what they were doing. He came around a corner and met my eyes. At first, I didn't think I'd ever seen him before, but after a few seconds of searching his face, I realized I had.

This was a face I had seen on the battlefield. It was early in the war, one of the first battles when the courts had only just been tossed into turmoil and few really understood what was happening. Only those at the top of the hierarchy knew the extent of the initial attacks that started the conflict, or the full horror of the aftermath. I was still reeling from it when we took the field that day. My mind was still racing when that face, the face that was staring back at me now, turned to me. It was streaked with blood and caked with dirt, but the eyes were unmistakable.

In that context I would have expected them to be filled with anger and hatred, but they weren't. His stare was vacant, empty, as if he had lost everything that was once inside him and was now fueled only by the commands directing his every move. On the ground at his feet was a man I had known all my life, had trusted and relied on. Then, he'd run before I could go after him that day. Now his eyes were locked on me, waiting for what I was going to do.

The same flicker of recognition went through him but he knew there was nothing I could do, standing where we were. Inside a human shop in the full view of the people browsing the displays was no place for us to reveal ourselves. If I tried anything it would only cause more trouble. He knew that and he was enjoying every second of my torment. It amused him that he was within feet of me, only a few steps away, and I could do absolutely nothing to exact the revenge he deserved.

"Is there something I could help you gentlemen find?"

I turned toward the sound of the voice and saw a concerned-looking young man standing behind me. His hands clasped tightly in front of him, he was looking back and forth between us like he hadn't had enough coffee that morning to manage a brawl breaking out in the middle of the quiet shop.

"No," I told him, turning back to the Fae man so he could see my eyes and not mistake my intentions. "I was just leaving."

My surroundings blurred as I walked back through the town toward the hotel. I knew the hours ahead of me would be long and stressful, but they would pass, and when they did, this would all come to an end. Seeing the Fae men in the bookshop and then again had heightened the feelings inside me, distilling them down to one painful but clear decision.

I was intensely, inexplicably drawn to Kip and my protective instincts toward her were only getting in my way. There was no more time to think. I had to defend my people and stop the war.

I had to kill Kip.

CHAPTER 5

Kip

"You know, you could have asked Mac to give you your birthday off rather than today," Harley said as we walked along the paved path leading into the park. "It would have actually given you a day to relax. But, you know, choices."

"Today is my regular day off," I pointed out to her. "You know how much he likes to keep to a schedule. Besides, the weather is much better today than it was on my birthday. There's no way we would have been able to come out here and enjoy the park. We would have melted before we made it out of the parking lot. Just think of it this way: now we get to celebrate my birthday twice."

She looked over at me through lashes heavy with mascara. "Because nothing says 21st birthday like a pleasant stroll through the park."

"We can go down to the lake and feed the geese." I held out the bag of bread remnants and leftover crackers.

"Partying hard, Kip. Partying hard."

Even as she said it, she grinned. Harley knew as well as I did that if we had grown up in any other circumstances, there would be no reason for us to be friends. But we were both extremely grateful that we were. We'd gotten each other through hard times and continued to carry one another. I knew I could always trust her. Even when it felt like there was no one else in the world who understood me, I knew I had her.

"I've been meaning to talk to you about something," I said as we got past the families gathered at the entrance and moved further into the peaceful park.

"What's up?" she asked.

"Have you noticed…" I suddenly felt ridiculous. "You know what, never mind."

"What?" Harley asked. "Have I noticed what?"

"I feel stupid for even bringing it up, but have you noticed a somewhat odd uptick in the amount of male attention I've been getting the last few days?"

"Are you talking about the long-haired guy who commandeered you in the bookshop yesterday?"

"He's part of it," I admitted.

"Good, because he's coming this way."

"What?" I hissed, whipping my head back to search the rolling grassy fields on either side of us. "Where?"

"Right there." She gestured with her head at the path to one side.

Sure enough, there he was. As sleek and sexy as before, in another precisely tailored suit, this time with his hair flowing free past his shoulders as he strode purposefully toward us. My heart rate quickened and I swallowed hard. I tried to keep my expression neutral, not wanting Harley to notice the effect he had on me.

"What in the hell is going on?" I asked under my breath.

"Hello," he said when he got to within a few steps of us.

"Hello," Harley and I answered in unison.

"It's a lovely day," he said.

"It is," I agreed.

We had only interacted with each other two times and already we'd evolved into small talk about the weather. I didn't know if that was a good sign or not. Confused as I was, I felt strangely happy to see him, and he was looking at me like he didn't notice anything else in the world. He didn't even acknowledge Harley, which was very rare. Harley stood out.

"I realized I never actually introduced myself," he said. "I'm Stryder." He took another step toward me and extended his hand. My skin tingled when I grasped it and he gave mine a squeeze rather than shaking it. We held hands longer than was normal and Harley cleared her throat, bumping my hip with hers.

"Oh, sorry." I reluctantly released his hand. "And this is Harley."

"It's very nice to meet you," he said. "Officially." He still didn't tear his gaze away from me.

I nodded and out of the corner of my eye I noticed Harley's gaze flickering back and forth between us. Her fingers wrapped around the plastic of the bag in my hand and yanked it away, holding it up so Stryder could see it.

"It's getting on toward the geese's lunchtime, and I hear they get pretty grumpy if they're left waiting. So I'm going to go ahead and head over to the lake. See you." She scurried away faster than I'd ever seen her move, especially towards any bird feeding opportunity available, and I turned awkwardly toward Stryder. He didn't seem at all put out by Harley's sudden departure. Instead, there was a slight smile on his lips.

"How about that walk?"

"I thought the point of the walk was to get some fresh air away from all the desperation," I teased.

"I'm sure we could find somebody to give us the right atmosphere, if that's what you need."

His smooth, dry sense of humor made him even more

attractive and before I even realized what I was doing, I had fallen into step beside him. I felt small next to him, not only in size but his mere presence commanded respect. I let the energy of it guide me as we walked along the path, away from the direction Harley had gone.

"Are you new to Glendale?" I asked after a few long moments of silence between us.

It was an utterly stupid question. Of course he was new to Glendale. If he wasn't, I would have noticed him well before now. But it was what had popped out of my mouth, so I went with it.

"Just visiting," he told me.

"What brought you here?" I asked.

"Business."

"You're a sparkling conversationalist," I told him.

Stryder looked down at me, his eyebrow quirking upward. "Is that so?"

I nodded, biting my lip to keep from smiling.

"Well then, now that you know something about me, what about you? Tell me about yourself."

"Well, I am not new to Glendale. I've been here my whole life. At least, my whole life that I remember."

"What does that mean?" he asked.

"I don't actually have any memories of the first few years of my life," I told him. "My parents adopted me when I was a little girl, but I don't remember where I was born or anything before being in the foster system."

I had no idea why I was telling him any of that. It wasn't exactly the most compelling of conversation topics. It was definitely not something I frequently dove right into with someone I had only just met. It's not that I was ashamed of my history. It was what it was, and it's not like I could do anything about it. Jumping into it with new people, though, was usually a bit of a downer.

"That's an interesting origin story," he said.

I glanced up at him and laughed.

"Origin story? You make it sound like I'm a superhero," I said.

"Are you?" he asked.

"Not that I know of, but I was a late bloomer so you never know. I could develop superpowers at any time," I told him.

I looked to the side and rolled my eyes. Stryder noticed the gesture.

"What's wrong?" he asked.

"Remember that guy from the bookshop yesterday?" I asked. "He came up while we were talking?"

"Yes," Stryder nodded, frowning.

"It seems he's having some trouble taking a hint," I said, pointing across the grass to where the man was sitting on a blanket openly staring at us.

"Isn't that another of the men who was there yesterday?" Stryder asked, gesturing toward a figure walking across the grass on the other side of the path.

I let out an exasperated sigh and nodded. "That would be another one of my fan club."

"You have a fan club?"

"Apparently. Not really. It's just really strange that since my birthday the other day these guys have been everywhere."

The near-constant presence of the strange men was really starting to make me uncomfortable. They barely tried to hide the way they were watching me. Instead, it felt like they wanted me to know they were there. It was unnerving.

Stryder surprised me by slipping his arm around my shoulders and steering me around a curve in the path.

"Come on," he said. "We'll get rid of them."

His touch made the tingling sensation in my stomach heighten. I held my breath, pinching myself. Was this really happening. *To me?*

He kept his arm around me until I could no longer turn around and see the men. We fell back into the small-talk conversation as he asked me the traditional getting-to-know-you questions, but offering almost no details about himself in return. The farther we walked, the shorter and more tense his responses were, and by the time we stopped I'd answered his one-word question with a story about the one and only dog I had owned in my life.

Our steps slowed and I realized we had made our way beyond the paved paths. We were onto the barely used dirt trails that skirted the back portion of the park. The smell of honey-suckle was strong from a thicket of trees surrounding the area and I took a few moments to breathe it in. I opened my eyes, gasping when I saw the elaborate dagger grasped in his hand as he came toward me.

CHAPTER 6

Stryder

Kip's eyes widened in fear as they locked on the dagger. Regret pounded into me. I growled, steeling myself. This was what I had to do. My family, my people, the whole Fae world depended on me. I couldn't let them down. And yet, I hesitated.

The fear in her eyes and my intense need to protect her, even from myself, made me still.

A flash of movement from the corner of my eye drew my attention. A figure appeared behind her and, in one swift movement, the Fae man swept his arms around Kip and lifted her off her feet. This was a man from the Summer Court, a servant of my enemy.

"Put her down!"

His eyes met mine and realization flashed through them. I surged at him, roaring. He held her tightly with one arm, yanking her out of the way. I crashed into him and we tumbled to the ground. There were a few tense seconds of tangled grappling before Kip pulled herself free. I jumped to my feet, pushing Kip behind me as I grabbed him by the scruff and yanked him off the ground, shaking him. Yelping, he stumbled backwards, pulling himself free of my hold. He knew he wouldn't be able to get her away from me and took off running.

"Stryder," she gasped. "What the hell was that?"

Tucking my dagger out of sight again, I ran after the man.

When I first saw the men in the bookshop, I knew what they were. My first thought was that they were in the human world for me. The Summer Queen knew I was her greatest threat and it would make sense for her to send assassins to eliminate the threat. It was obvious now that wasn't the case. They weren't tracking me. They were here for Kip. They had the same prophecy.

The wizards had warned me that she was a powerful force and represented how this war would unfold.

Though nothing more than a human with no ties to my world, she was inexplicably valuable. She would be the one to ensure the Summer Queen continued on her evil campaign through The Land of Sidhe.

I had come to destroy her.

But not these men.

They wouldn't want anything to happen to the woman who would ensure their queen's ascent to full and unchallenged power. There were plans in place for her and I wanted to know what those plans were.

The man's speed was no match for mine and I quickly caught up with him. My hand wrapped tightly around the back of his shirt and I spun him around, slamming him against a tree. His feet were barely touching the ground and the pressure of my forearm against the front of his neck was enough to keep him exactly where I wanted.

At at my mercy.

"I hope you aren't expecting me to bow down to you, King," the man growled through gritted teeth.

He struggled against my grip on him, but I forced him

harder against the tree. His eyes closed and he hissed as the rough bark cut into his skin.

"Who are you?" I demanded.

His eyes opened slowly, displaying the glistening black and bitterness behind them.

"You don't recognize me?" he asked. "I suppose that shouldn't surprise me. Why would the king concern himself with remembering a lowly servant like Keilen?"

The name triggered something in the back of my mind. I could hear it being spoken by a voice that made my veins burn and my edges of my vision go red.

"Keilen," I muttered. "Still simpering at the feet of the Queen. Didn't she humiliate you enough?"

His eyes hardened even more and I knew he was remembering the same night I was, the last time the monarchs of the courts had come together in some semblance of peace.

That was before the war, when the whispers of the Summer Queen's cruelty and her plans for total power were still just rumors. She hadn't yet made her first move. That was the night she cast Keilen, one of her attendants, to the floor and screamed at him because he accidentally spilled water onto her gown. She'd finished the assault by pouring the rest of the water onto his head.

"My queen expects nothing but the very best," he spat back at me. "Only her most loyal will be favored when she ascends to the ultimate throne."

"Do you really believe that?" I asked. "Or are you only telling yourself that because it's the only way you can survive?"

"You will never beat her. You aren't strong enough and you don't have what she does."

I lifted him up higher and slammed him against the tree again. This part of the conversation was over.

"What are you doing here?" I asked forcefully.

"I could ask the same of you. Don't you think you should be

back in our world? The Blood Court needs all the help it can get." He grinned, making my stomach churn. "You know they won't be able to hold out against our forces much longer."

"You don't know what you're talking about," I told him. "Why are you here? Why are you following Kip?"

"Kip, is it? The human girl has a name. It surprises me that you would know it, King Stryder. I think you have far better things to worry about than her."

"And you don't?" I asked.

"What I'm doing and why I'm here is none of your concern."

"It is when it has to do with her," I growled.

The protectiveness and need to defend Kip became a primal urge inside me. It felt like a burning mass in my belly that sent fire up into my chest. Just the thought of him being anywhere near her was enough to make me want to snap every bone in his body.

Knowing that he'd even touched her made me want scream. To cut off the hands that had touched her and remove the eyes that had dared look at her. The fact that he dared speak about her made me want to destroy him.

A sudden and unexpected realization settled into me and I dropped him to his feet. Shocked, I stumbled backwards.

He started to say something but the crack of my knuckles into his face stopped him. He laughed. "King Stryder, debasing himself by fighting a servant. Is this how you plan on winning the war?"

I punched him again, this time hard enough to send him crashing to the ground. I kicked him hard in the side to flip him onto his back and dropped down to press my knee into the center of his chest so he could do nothing but stare up at me.

"No," I said low in my throat. "But it is how I will defend *her*."

The hard jolt of his bent knee hit me in the side, catching me off-guard. I released the pressure of my knee on his chest, falling sideways. He immediately surged up to knock me over onto the ground. He came down on me and we grappled, using our fists, elbows, and knees to pound into each other. We both would have been more comfortable using some of our magic, but that wasn't an option. Utilizing powers in the human world was far too risky.

Even without my magic, the servant was no match for me. He was fighting to defend his own honor, in the name of the vicious queen. She'd manipulated him into being loyal. That was nothing in comparison to what fueled me. It was what gave me strength and energy, but also what stopped me before utterly destroying him. Kip.

The sound of her voice calling my name brought my fist back away from Keilen's face. In the brief moment, he forced me away and scrambled to his feet. Wiping blood away from his mouth, he locked eyes with me.

"I will be back for her," he said bitterly. "I swear to you, you won't keep me from her."

He turned and disappeared, running into the trees. I wanted to follow him, but instead I turned around and headed in the direction of Kip's voice. It was clear now what was making my mission so impossibly difficult, and what force was drawing me to her. It wasn't that she was innocent and unassuming.

Kip was my fated mate.

The realization hit me so hard it was hard for me to think, to breathe. Her voice called out again and I rushed toward her. What if she was in trouble again? She wasn't just a human woman. She wasn't just a face, a being, a player in the war that I had to end.

Kip was the woman destined for me.

We were crafted specifically to be together and would have been drawn irresistibly to one another even if the wizards hadn't sent me here.

They had no idea. They couldn't. If those men, my most trusted advisers, had any indication of who Kip was and what she was meant to be in my life, they never would have told me to come.

Now I was caught in an impossible situation, torn between two parts of myself.

I must either kill the being who would destroy my kingdom. Or save the woman who was my fated mate.

As I came over a hill, I saw Kip in front of me. Harley was with her, her arm wrapped tightly around Kip's shoulders. Wide green eyes met mine and, in that instant, a snap decision took over.

"He didn't hurt you, did he?" I approached them, eyes roaming over her to ensure she was okay.

Kip shook her head, the movement causing some of her wild curls to stick to the dampness on her cheek. I fought the urge to brush it away.

"I can't believe you saw him," she said. "You scared me so much with that knife."

My spine tensed and Harley's dark eyes searched me.

"I'm just glad I was there," I said. "Where do you live?"

There was no time to try to come up with a smoother way to ease into the conversation. Keilen would live up to his promise and come after us, likely with a whole army of men by his side. We had to run.

CHAPTER 7

Kip

I was still shaking. It felt like the outside of my body had gotten ahold of itself, but the inside was still trembling. Harley's arm around my shoulders was comforting, even if it was a touch tighter than it needed to be. She looked around with every step, as if she was waiting for the man to come running out of the trees to scoop me up again. Even as Stryder approached, she pulled me in closer and eased me slightly behind her.

"What were you doing with a knife?" she asked.

He didn't even look at her. Icy blue eyes stayed trained on me like he didn't care about anything else. Instead, his stare burned into me, making my heart thump wildly in my chest.

"Where do you live?" he repeated.

"Why?" My voice came out a squeak.

"I'll take you home." His voice was firm, as if there was no room for argument.

"Should we call the police?" I asked. "Maybe we should tell them what happened." Suddenly my mind cleared and I noticed something about Stryder's face. "You're bleeding." I stepped up closer, reaching for the narrow trickle coming from the corner of his mouth. There was something strange about the blood, but before I could touch it to look closer, he dodged my touch and wiped it away.

"I'm fine." His eyebrows narrowed, creating a stern look. So handsome, so mysterious. He's fought that man, to keep me safe. Color me intrigued as hell.

"You found him?" Harley asked.

Now Stryder looked over at her. He gave an almost imperceptible nod.

"Don't call the police," he said. "He already got away."

"He might still be around," I said. "He could be dangerous to someone else in the park."

Stryder's shoulders lowered as he let out a breath. "He's not going to be dangerous to anyone else. You need to get home."

"Listen to him," Harley told me.

"Excuse me?" My eyes swung over to her. "Did you just *agree* with someone?"

Harley rolled her eyes. "Don't get used to it. But he's making sense. It's hot as hell out here and you just went through something traumatic. You don't need to be hanging around here talking to a bunch of police who aren't going to be able to do anything about it. We'll get you back to your house and let you relax for a bit, then we'll call them."

I nodded. Part of me still thought we should tell someone what happened, but they were right. I really didn't want to be in the park. The idea of being back home in the air conditioning and not feeling like a thousand eyes were on me was very appealing.

"Let's go," I said.

We walked back through the park toward the tiny parking lot.

"My car is a few blocks away," Harley said. "There was no space, so I had to park down the other street."

"Do you want a ride to it?" I asked.

She shook her head.

"Don't worry about it. I'll be right behind you," she said.

If I knew Harley, and I did, she would *not* head directly towards her car. Instead, she was going to scour every corner and shady spot for the man who attacked me. Considering the blood on Stryder's face and the bruising showing up on his hands, I couldn't imagine it would be too difficult to identify the guy if he was still strolling around.

"See you there," I said, accepting her hug.

Stryder's pace sped up until I was nearly in a jog beside him. I directed him to my beat-up Mustang. It was so old, the red paint had faded into a pink shade.

"Give me your keys." He held his hand towards me.

I was startled by the intensity in his voice but shook my head. "Actually, I think I'm going to be fine," I told him. "It would make me feel better to just drive myself. Thanks."

He gave a curt nod. I expected him to leave me here but, before I could thank him for saving me, he climbed into my passenger seat. "I'm still going with you."

I stared at him as he struggled to fold himself in the front seat of my 'Stang. He looked ridiculous, too large and masculine in the rusted, pink car. I tried not to laugh but it was very difficult. I also didn't feel like arguing with him, and if I was being really honest, it was comforting to have him there. Not that I thought anyone was going to jump up out of the backseat at me or anything, but his presence made me feel better.

We were silent as I drove through the town and into the neighborhood where I'd lived since I was adopted.

I was *very* aware of Stryder in the seat beside me. A tension buzzed between us, unspoken but just as lively as a hot wire. His hand rested on the console, so near me, and I wanted him to reach out and touch me. Take my hand. It was a childish desire, especially compared to his manliness. Just the thought of it made my hands sweat and I wiped them on my jeans. He seemed to take up more of the car than his body should and my eyes kept sliding to the side to look at him. The temperature was creeping up and we reached for the vent at the same time. Our hands touched and my body tingled. He pulled his hand away quickly, but I could see him looking at me out of the corner of his eye, like he was evaluating the feelings becoming stronger between us.

"This is me," I said, pulling into a narrow driveway, grateful the car ride was over.

"Your house?" Stryder asked.

I nodded. Answering the question felt funny, almost like I was a little girl still playing make-believe.

"Yes. It's still strange to think of it that way. My father passed more than a year ago, and my mom died when I was fifteen, but I still think of it as their house," I told him.

"I'm sorry to hear that," he said.

His actions didn't exactly underscore the apology. The words were barely out of his mouth when he climbed out of the car and started to the front door in long, determined strides. Somewhat confused, I followed him. Stryder barely stepped aside enough to let me get the door unlocked before he went through and into the living room.

"Come on in," I said as I followed him inside and shut the door behind me.

Either he didn't catch the sarcasm in my voice or didn't care about it. Stryder stood in the middle of the room and looked around, then stalked into the dining room. He ducked his head into the kitchen leading off to one side, then disappeared into it.

"What's in here?" he asked.

"Are you looking for something in particular?" I asked, walking into the kitchen.

"What's in here?" he repeated, pointing at the white-painted door on one wall.

"Oh, that?" I asked. Lowering my eyelashes, I took a few steps toward him, adding a little extra sway to my hips. I dropped my voice. "That's where I do something very, very *dirty.*" His eyes were instantly on me, dark and dangerous, swirling with emotions. Blatant, heated lust. It made my breath hitch as another step brought me nearly against him. I dropped my voice to a sultry whisper. "My laundry."

Frowning, he blinked, and then the heated look dissolved into a something more confused.

He yanked the door open and I laughed when he saw my washer and dryer and rolled his eyes. Slamming the door shut, he stalked back out of my kitchen and down the hall leading toward the bathroom and two bedrooms that made up the rest of this floor of the house. He walked into my bedroom and some of the laughter died in my throat.

"Do you have a suitcase?"

"What?" That was definitely a question that needed some more investigation. I hurried through the dining room and down the hallway into my room. He already had two of my dresser drawers open and was leaning into my closet.

"What the hell do you think you're doing?" I asked, slamming my drawers shut.

He stepped right up behind me and opened them again, reaching in for handfulls of clothes.

"Get your suitcase," he said.

"Why would I do that?" I asked.

"Because you're in danger," he answered.

"Okay. I think it's right about time for that call to the police," I said.

Stryder reached out and grabbed my wrist before I could get out of the room. In the back of my mind, I knew this was one of those moments in my life that should scare me. It should have been fear going through me rather than curiosity. Yet I didn't move. His eyes met mine without hesitation and I could see the sincerity in them. I tried to breathe, but it felt like the air was caught in my throat. The warmth from where his hand touched my skin radiated through my body and my awareness of everything else around me faded. His touch became the epicenter of my concentration, of my focus. My heart was beating hard enough against my ribs I was sure he could hear it this time. Finally, his voice broke the haze.

"Not in danger from me," he said. "And if you just tell me where the suitcase is, I'll get it myself."

"There's a duffel bag on the top shelf," I pulled my wrist from his hand before pointing to the closet. "But I still don't understand what's going on."

He crossed the room in one stride and reached up to pull down the gray and navy bag I'd dragged with me to my grandmother's house for sleepovers and the one fateful summer in high school my parents thought it would be a good idea to send me to summer camp. It had been sitting on that shelf ever since, just waiting for some other purpose for existing. Maybe waiting for this.

"We need to leave," Stryder said. "Get your clothes together, your toothbrush, whatever it is you'll need to be away for a while."

"Are we going to summer camp?" I crossed my arms across my chest, tapping my foot. "If so, be sure to grab the bug repellant."

"Look," he said, tossing a handful of clothes from another drawer onto the bed, "we really don't have the time to go back and forth about this. Get your stuff together so we can leave."

"You expect me to just go along with you? I'm supposed to skip off with you to lord only knows where because you said so?" I asked.

"I'm telling you that you need to do this because you do, and you just need to trust that," he said.

"What's going on?" Harley's voice rang through the room. I

looked toward the door to the bedroom to see her standing there staring in at us.

I pointed at Stryder. "Apparently he and I are getting ready to ride off into the sunset together. I'll send postcards."

"What are you talking about?" Harley asked, stepping angrily into the room. "Are you seriously leaving?"

"Of course I'm not leaving," I told her.

"Yes, she is," Stryder said.

He opened the top drawer of my dresser and pulled out a handful of panties.

"Okay," I said, swiping him away from the dresser and snatching everything back from him, "I don't need you manhandling my delicates." Seeing Stryder gripping my favorite lace boy shorts was just too much for my mind to wrap around in that moment.

"I don't know who you think you are, but you're not just going to take her," Harley said. "She's not going anywhere with you."

"It doesn't matter who I am," Stryder said back, his voice simmering. "She is going with me because staying here is putting her life at risk."

CHAPTER 8

Stryder

Ugh. Human women were ridiculous. Baffling. Frustrating. I longed to be back in my Kingdom, where everyone followed and obeyed. So much easier than dealing with these humans.

Couldn't they see that Kip was in danger? Sure, I might be misleading them somewhat. It was true that Kip staying here was going to put her life at serious risk. But coming with me could be just as dangerous. The reality of the men from the Summer Court coming for her only underscored the urgency of my mission. I couldn't let them get their hands on her.

It was also true that her life wouldn't be in immediate danger with those men. They were trying to kidnap her, not kill her. But as revered as she would be for the role she would play in winning the war, she would also be disposable. As soon as she had exhausted her usefulness, they'd cast her aside. Knowing the Summer Queen, at that point, death might be welcome. She'd never tolerate anyone else being seen as more important than her. She would present Kip as a critical game piece in public, but behind closed doors ensure Kip never forgot her true place.

As for me, I still withered between my duty and my desire. The primal need to protect her was still there. I knew who she was and the inextricable power that held. But that didn't change the cold, bitter reality of my responsibility to my people. As king, I was sworn from birth to put them above myself for the good of the kingdom. That meant making any sacrifice necessary to protect them. It was something I had always taken seriously and devoted myself to fully, never expecting the degree of sacrifice that might be asked of me.

I knew I didn't have much time to make the choice. I couldn't just take Kip and run forever. There would be a moment soon when I would have to decide whether to take her life or find another way to defend those of my own kind.

But that would come later. For right now, it was time to convince a stubborn, headstrong woman that she was, in fact, in danger.

Currently, she was staring me down, hand on her hip, a determined look on her face. Lords, her spark was attractive. It brought out the protective warrior in me, the one who wanted to throw her over my shoulder and carry her back to the safety of my castle.

"That is the second time you've made some not-so-subtle references to people wanting to take me out," she said. "I'll admit, that last guy was a bit of an escalation. But, that doesn't change the fact that you need to tell me what's going on."

"I'll tell you on the way." Ignoring my instincts to grab her, cave-man style, I stuffed a few more pieces of clothing into her bag.

She shoved her hand over it, blocking my way and I huffed, looking up at her. She met my gaze with a steely one of her own. "No. You're going to tell me now."

How adorable. "Where's your toothbrush?" She crossed her arms over her chest defiantly, not answering. I strode out of the room and into the bathroom across the hall, then back to the bedroom, holding it out. "A pink plastic cup on your bathroom sink isn't exactly lockdown."

"Damn," she muttered when she saw her toothbrush disappear into a corner of the bag.

"I am familiar with the man who tried to take you," I said.

Kip's arms loosened and fell to her sides as Harley's eyes flashed with anger.

"You *know* that guy?" she demanded.

"I don't *know* him. I know *of* him."

"And the others?" Kip asked. "All those other men squirming around the bookshop and popping up out of nowhere all over town?"

"I'm familiar with them," I confirmed.

"What is that supposed to mean? What do you mean you're *familiar* with them?"

"Exactly what I said. There isn't time to get into it right now."

"Is this why you didn't want me to call the police?"

"Yes. They wouldn't be able to do any good."

"I'm not going to be doing any badge-kissing any time soon," Harley said, "but their job is to keep people safe. An attempted kidnapping requiring a big-ass knife to ward the guy off is one of those types of situations."

I looked over at Kip and she nodded slightly. "Harley has a bit of a checkered history with the law."

"They can only do that job if they know what they are facing, and right now, they don't. Kip is going to be safest with me."

"Stryder..."

She didn't look convinced and I stepped up closer to her. I reached out and took both of her hands, knowing touching her was going to make this all even harder for me, but needing her to focus on me. Our eyes met and I held them.

"Kip, please. I know you have no reason to, but I need you to trust me."

She stared back at me for a few seconds without pulling away.

"You can't seriously be considering this," Harley said incredulously.

"I don't know why I'm doing this…" she started.

"Then *don't*," Harley said.

"You're sure about this?" Kip asked, looking at me intently.

"Yes."

She took a breath and let it out slowly, then gave a sharp nod.

"Good enough for me," I reached for the duffel bag, but Harley snatched it off the bed before my hand wrapped around the handle.

"You're not taking her."

"It isn't up to you," I told her.

"I'm not going to let you take off with her and not have any idea where she is or when I'll see her again."

She dug her heels in and wasn't going to budge. I could either stand here and waste more time arguing with her, or I could force her hand.

"Then you're going to have to come with us."

"What?"

"You said you're not going to let me take off with her and not have any idea where she is. So you'll have to come with us. It would be better anyway. Your presence alone could put Kip in more danger."

"Why would you say that?" Kip asked.

I sighed, wishing I could just magic them away right now. It would be a lot easier. What was that human saying? It's easier to ask for forgiveness later than permission now. I was seriously considering the whole 'throwing her over my shoulder' thing. Instead, I tried to explain. "She could be used to get to you. She already knows too much. Those men didn't just show up. They've been watching you. They may have been here even

longer than I have, and they will know the two of you are close."
I turned to Harley. "Once they figure out that Kip is missing, they're going to do whatever it takes to get to her, and that includes coming after you for the information. Without you here, it won't be as easy for them to find us."

"Fine," Harley responded without hesitation.

"Then you better hurry and get what you need. We've already wasted enough time."

We headed out of the house and my heart gave an unexpected, painful squeeze when Kip turned around and locked her door. In that moment, she had no idea when she might come back to her home. I didn't know if she ever would.

Harley waved her hand to get our attention as we made our way toward Kip's car.

"Let's use mine," she said.

"Why?" Kip asked.

"If he's right and these guys have been watching you long enough that they know who I am, they are going to be able to recognize your car. You haven't been in my car with me except for once in the last few weeks, so it would be harder for them to identify it."

"She's right," I agreed. "These men have ways of tracking and finding the people and things they want to find. Anything we can do to hold them off is going to be valuable."

"Be careful," Harley said as she climbed in behind the wheel of the weathered eggplant-colored compact car. "You just got dangerously close to saying something nice about me."

"Don't get used to it."

We made our way to an apartment building and Harley took only a few moments inside before coming out with a bag thrown over her shoulder.

"Is that everything you need?" I asked.

"I travel light," she said. "You get used to it after being shuffled around."

I remembered what Kip had told me about the two of them growing up in foster care and nodded.

"I'd like to point out I have no idea what's in my bag," Kip said. "Going by the only evidence I gathered, there's about twelve T-shirts, a toothbrush, and a handful of panties."

"You took the panties and stuffed them back in the drawer," Harley said.

"Oh, damn. I did. I have no panties."

"That's the least of our worries," I said.

"That's true. Which brings me to a somewhat pressing question... where are we going?"

I shook my head. "I don't know."

"You don't know? We're just going to wander where the wind takes us?"

"Right now all that matters is getting you away from this town and those men. The one who grabbed you told me he would be coming back for you. By the speed he was hurrying away, it's guaranteed he won't be coming back alone. The faster we can get away, the better off we'll be."

Taking Kip out of Glendale was the only thing on my mind. It didn't matter where we went as long as we could stay ahead of the men from the Summer Court until I could make my decision. When I told the women the men had a way of tracking the people they wanted to find, I'm sure their thoughts immediately went to technology and any number of gadgets that could narrow it down. It was so much more than that.

The queen's choice of men wasn't accidental or random. She would have selected men with specific skills, knowing the critical importance of them finding Kip quickly. That meant those men likely had tracking powers. It would be hard to escape them.

But not impossible, and I was determined to keep her safe... for now.

CHAPTER 9

Kip

Stryder took over driving less than an hour into the trip and the sun had long since set when he spoke again. Harley and I kept ourselves entertained singing and rehashing those old conversations that close friends like us could have a thousand times over. The sudden injection of his voice was startling.

"We'll go a few more hours."

I turned around in the passenger seat to look at Harley and then back at Stryder.

"Since you're volunteering answers to questions we didn't ask, why don't you answer one we do ask?" I asked.

"What is it that you want to know?"

"That is a very broad door you are opening for me to walk through," I told him. He stayed silent so I continued. "What did you mean when you said you are familiar with those men?"

"A real answer this time. Not another cutesy riddle," Harley warned.

"I don't know specifically who they are, but I know what they are."

"What they are? Creeps? The woefully socially inept? The Glendale branch of the Future Kidnappers of America Association?"

"Fae," he said.

The car went completely silent as I waited for him to keep going. That couldn't possibly be his entire answer. There had to be a continuation of that word or a link to an unfortunate sports mascot situation. But Stryder didn't say anything else.

"Fae?" I asked. "As in fairies?"

"That's not a term we like to throw around, but yes."

There was another brief stretch of silence.

"Stop the car," I said.

"What do you mean?"

"I mean stop the car. I just realized how insane I am, and how delusional you are. It's crazy enough for you to convince me to leave with you, but now you're driving out in middle of nowhere talking about being a fairy. I want to get off this ride. There is not enough Dramamine in the existence of the world to make it tolerable."

"I'm not stopping the car. Like you said, we're out in the middle of nowhere. I'm not just going to pull off by the side of the road and let you out. Besides, you need to listen to me. There are a few things you need to hear."

"Are you building up to tell me Tinkerbell's in the glove compartment and you want me to let her out?"

"I would hope you could tell just by looking at me that we're not exactly talking about the same species. That's exactly why we prefer to avoid the word fairy."

"That's understandable," Harley said.

"Let's pretend, just for a second, that I am going to entertain your little flight of fancy here. Why would a bunch of *Fae* men come to Glendale? There has to be plenty of far more interesting things to see and do in Fairyland. I'm sorry. Faeworld."

"The Land of Sidhe."

"The what?" I asked.

"The Land of Sidhe. What it's called. The home of my kind."

"It has a lovely ring to it. But at the risk of repeating myself, why would those men, or you for that matter, come to Glendale? When I first met you, you said it was for business."

"It is, in a way. We didn't just randomly end up in Glendale. We went there because you were there. That's why it's so important for you to trust me. You are in extreme danger because of those men. There's a war happening in my world and there's strong evidence you might have something to do with it."

"How could I possibly have something to do with a war in a world I didn't even know existed? That I'm still very much doubting exists?"

"You doubting it or not has nothing to do with whether it's real, or your significance. My highest advisors told me to look for you. That's enough to verify to me without any hesitation that you are the person I believe you are."

"Are these other not-fairies?" Harley asked.

"Wizards," Stryder told her.

"And that's my limit. My disbelief can suspend no longer. This has been lovely, but I'm going to have to ask you to stop," I said again.

"I'm still not stopping. This is a lot for you to take in, but you're going to have to try to absorb it as quickly as you can. Your world is about to change more than you can imagine."

"I think it already has."

"Far more are coming. The more you know and understand about it, the better chances you have of survival."

"You seem to really enjoy trying to scare the pants off me, but answer this for me. How am I supposed to know we can trust you? You yourself just admitted that those men are your kind."

"They are from the same species, but that doesn't make them

the same. Those men are from the Summer Court. Their queen is who started this war."

"And you?" I asked.

"I'm from the Blood Court."

"Well, isn't that wholesome," Harley said.

"It's the responsibility of my court to trace the lineage and history of the Fae."

None of this was sinking into my head fully. Usually I'm the type of person who's willing to take a bit of a leap when it comes to believing in the impossible. My childhood instilled in me two almost directly opposing characteristics. The time bouncing around in foster care, then watching Harley wait for an adoption that never happened, made it hard for me to trust people. It gave me a knee-jerk reaction to questioning the sincerity and motivations of just about anybody who crossed my path. On the other hand, being adopted into an absolutely incredible family taught me to suspend my disbelief when faced with something that seemed completely out of the realm of possibility.

But even I was struggling with this one.

"That doesn't really mean anything. You went to Glendale to find me just the same as they did. You admitted it. How am I supposed to know you're actually any different from them?"

"I saved you from being kidnapped," he said, sounding offended.

"If you really want to get technical with this, you are currently saving me from being kidnapped *by kidnapping me.*"

"That is not what's happening," Stryder insisted. "I am not kidnapping you."

"Really? Because it really seems to me like you are bringing us to some undisclosed location without our consent. That's kidnapping."

"It seems like you have a memory problem, because you did give your consent." I opened my mouth to argue with him but just made an unintelligible noise, because, unfortunately, he was right. His upper lip quivered upwards in humor. "Not telling you where we're going just makes it a fun surprise."

"That is a very fancy precedent you just set."

"What if he's a part of it?" Harley suddenly asked from the backseat. "Kip, I'm serious. Did you even think about that?"

"What are you talking about?"

"He's not some separate entity from those men, playing vigilante through Glendale and rescuing damsels in distress. He was a part of this all along. Think about it. He just conveniently showed up at the park the same time we were there? Then I walked away from the two of you for five seconds and he lures you into some dicey back corner?"

"To be fair, you did take the bird food and run." I turned towards her. "Something tells me you weren't exactly planning on only being away for five seconds."

"And that worked out well for him. He has been acting like he's just a visitor to town, but somehow he knew how to access one of the back areas where no one else goes? Then, conveniently, that is also the spot where that guy happens to jump out at you. He knew what was coming. He knew that guy was going to jump on you and he was prepared with his knife to scare him off. But it was all a ruse so he could get you to voluntarily climb into a car and go with him. It's all a big conspiracy."

"What about you?" I asked.

"Bonus," she said.

"That is *not* what's happening," Stryder snapped. "I told you their kind has ways of tracking the things and people they want to find. They knew where she was."

"And the back corner of the park?"

"I walked until the path ended. That doesn't take any particular skill or extensive knowledge of the area."

"So, what are we actually doing now? What's the point of all this?"

"The tracking isn't perfect, and it works best in close proximity. If we can keep our distance and use as many back roads and complicated routes as we can, it will lessen the effect even further. The point is to keep you away from them as long as we possibly can."

"I just want to get out and go home," I said, suddenly feeling nostalgic for my home that was comforting and familiar.

"We have to keep going. It's the only way to keep you safe. Close your eyes for a while. I'll wake you when we stop."

It was obvious there wasn't going to be any sort of real resolution to the conversation. Stryder had tempted us with just enough information to keep us intrigued. My brain was still fighting to believe him, and I could tell by the look in Harley's eyes she wasn't convinced, either. But I knew we weren't going to get anything else out of him that night.

Deciding to take his advice, I unlatched my seatbelt and climbed into the backseat so I could stretch out more. Harley and I got as comfortable as possible and dozed off.

CHAPTER 10

Stryder

The glowing numbers on the dashboard clock told me it was getting close to midnight. We'd filled the gas tank during our stop shortly after leaving Kip's house and I'd been weaving through the back roads since. The progress was slower than it would have been if we'd headed for the highway, but I felt safer this way. The main roads were direct shots, easier to track. Many of the tiny passages we had taken didn't even have names. Instead, little wooden posts presented numbers at the entrances. I followed them without any specific plan or destination in mind, hoping we didn't dead end.

Eventually I'd have to put more purpose behind my driving than just getting Glendale behind us and making it as hard as possible for the Summer Fae to find us. With any luck, they would have lain low for a few hours after the botched kidnapping attempt at the park. That would put space and time between us. It wasn't a permanent solution. Even at a distance, their tracking ability would eventually zero in on Kip. The fervent devotion and madness of the queen's followers meant they wouldn't rest until they'd accomplished their purpose.

All we could do was ready ourselves.

Kip whimpered in the backseat and I glanced into the rearview mirror to check on her. Curled up with her head resting on the door, she looked small and vulnerable. Without her sharp tongue and pushing back against virtually everything I said when she was awake, it was even easier to see how fragile she really was. My hands tightened around the steering wheel and my teeth gritted in anger at the memory of the man grabbing her. The feeling melted a few seconds later when the memory was overtaken by another one. My palms tingled thinking of holding her hand. It was only for a few brief seconds, but the connection was powerful and only deepened the desire to shield her from harm.

Even if she hadn't resisted everything, telling her the truth was going to be difficult. The reality of who I was and what was waiting for her hit hard, but her total resistance frustrated me. I was dedicated to serving and protecting my people, but that didn't change the fact that I was king. Getting what I wanted was just part of my station.

Kip completely defied that.

She was spark and energy, bundled up into a little package and she saw my way as nothing more than a suggestion. A suggestion she more often than not rejected, at that.

Yet, I was fascinated by her. She was aggravating, stubborn, relentless, and godsdamn sexy. The adamant flare in her eyes made my own flare ignite in my body. Combined with my natural instinct to protect her, it was an explosive combination, burning me inside.

And yet, the unanswered decision hung over my head.

It wouldn't let me ignore it. Even as I turned, backtracked, and looped my way through the dark fields and loosely scattered buildings of the countryside, my responsibility was never far from my thoughts. The voices of my advisors were a constant stream in the back of my mind. They pulled no punches when it came to telling me how bleak the future of my world would be if the war continued. It wasn't just the brutality and loss of life happening on the battlefields. If the war continued to rage and the Summer Queen won, all was lost.

A world controlled completely by the queen was something none of us wanted to face. To describe it as unlivable would be unendingly generous. Her desire for power wasn't something new and none of her actions were rash or compulsive. She was nothing if not calculating. Years had passed since the first rumors of her plans turned into whispers that spread through the courts. She'd always been challenging and rarely cooperated smoothly with the rest of us. That made it easier to ignore what we all realized now was a building threat.

The stark reality was that if the queen had suddenly decided to invade or was making decisions in an instant, she would be like a flash of flame that could be easily extinguished. Instead, her craving to rule over all of the realms and see every creature beneath her was like a fire that burned deep underground. It spread far, infecting the land and taking over the thoughts and faculties of anyone she could get ahold of. By the time her plans came into action and she made her first act of war, the burn was so pervasive it seemed uncontrollable.

That's where I came in.

I had never fallen under her charm or been afraid of what would be revealed if that charm fell away. There was never even an instant of hesitation or questioning about standing in her way. No matter how insurmountable the challenge seemed, I was willing to face it. There hadn't been a second when I could imagine anything stopping me.

My gaze returned to the rearview mirror and Kip's peacefully sleeping face. The pain in my chest that had started earlier, and been my constant companion since, intensified. It never would have crossed my mind that I'd be called to give so much. I always would have said there was nothing I wouldn't do for my kingdom. Or that no decision would be difficult for me, if it meant knowing my people would be safe. Now it's like those words had come back to haunt me.

The safety, the very lives and futures of all the people in my kingdom and beyond, rested in my hands. I only had to decide if I was willing to live the rest of my life with those hands covered in the blood of my fated mate.

Kip whimpered again. She had been doing it since she fell asleep. I could only imagine it was a sound she always made, but this time it got louder and higher-pitched, like she was afraid. I looked behind me and saw her eyes squeezed tightly, her mouth open like she was trying to scream. Her body thrashed slightly, and one hand reached out. She grabbed onto the handle of the door and the feeling of something tangible in her grip shocked her awake. Her eyes locked onto mine.

"Are you all right?" I asked.

She stared at me in a daze, a flash of fear in her eyes. I was compelled to reach for her, to reassure her that she was safe with me. I slid my hand off the wheel but she shook her head, then nodded. "I'm fine. Just a nightmare."

Feeling disappointed, I put my hand back on the wheel. "What was it about?"

Her eyes moved slightly to the side, then came back to me. "I don't remember. It just felt like something really horrible was happening."

"There's some lights up ahead. That looks like maybe somewhere we can stop. The car is going to need more gas before we can keep going."

She groaned again, but it was one of aggravation rather than fear. "How much farther do we have to go? We've been driving for hours."

I didn't answer her, but pulled into the parking lot of the

vibrantly illuminated gas station. It was the first open business I'd seen in a long time. As much as I wanted to minimize the amount of time we were staying in one place, I was relieved to find it. The car was quickly getting low on fuel and the last thing we needed was to be stranded in the empty darkness somewhere. By then, all the food the women had gotten during our first stop was gone and I was sure they were going to need something else to keep them going. I had no appetite.

Kip nudged Harley when we parked. They unfolded themselves from the backseat and stretched. The night air was cool and seemed to give them a jolt of energy. Both started quickly toward the building and I rushed after them, not wanting Kip out of my sight. Just before they ducked into the bathroom, she reached into her pocket and handed me a handful of folded bills.

"Gas and snacks," she said.

She didn't elaborate and I stared at the closed bathroom door for a few seconds before turning into the shop. Several cramped aisles contained a dizzying array of snack foods and I browsed them as discerningly as I could. There was nothing to go on in my decision-making process but what the women had shown during our last stop. Unfortunately for me, only one of those foods was in stock.

Gripping the bag of cheese-stuffed pretzels, I turned down the next aisle to investigate rows of candy and sweets.

"I came here to stop a war and now I'm debating the virtues of cream-filled sponge cake versus licorice twists," I muttered to myself. "Perfect."

Finally, I gave up and grabbed several of the nearest items to carry up to the cashier. She looked about as energetic and enthusiastic as to be expected of someone working the night shift in the middle of nowhere. She perked up slightly as I approached the counter and I noticed her eyes traveling over my hair and into the opening of my shirt where I'd loosened two buttons for the drive.

"On a long road trip, honey?" she asked.

"It has turned out to be, yes."

"Where you headed?"

The door to the store opened and I instinctively looked over to see who was coming in. The man didn't look like any of the Fae we'd left behind. I also didn't recognize him as anyone else from my world. He avoided my gaze and walked toward the first aisle.

"I'm not sure," I said to the cashier.

"Not sure? Seems like you're getting an awful lot of snacks for one person not knowing where he's headed."

She said it with a crooked grin I likely would have recognized as an attempt at being alluring if my attention wasn't on the man now roaming down the aisle nearest to the bathroom door. His attention kept moving from the shelves of car supplies to the closed door and back, like he was waiting for the door to open or someone to come out.

"I'm not alone," I said absently to the cashier, still watching the man.

She let out a disgruntled *hmmph* and went to work tallying everything into the register. I reached behind me to set the money on the counter as the man took a few steps toward the bathroom. He reached into his pocket as the bathroom door opened. Harley stepped out first, turning to look over her shoulder and laughing at Kip as she came up behind. I sprinted down the aisle, my gut twisting. The man said something to Kip and drew something out of his pocket. Light glinted off the metal in his hand and I ran into him, my hand gripping his throat. I threw his back to the wall, almost before I realized I was moving.

"What do you think you're doing?" I seethed.

The metal object hit the floor and skittered across the cracked linoleum.

"Stryder, stop! Let him go," Kip commanded from beside me.

Harley slipped past us and moved toward the front of the store, but I didn't pay attention to where she was going.

"What do you want with Kip?"

The man's eyes flickered back and forth rapidly.

"With *who?*"

"What do you mean with who?"

"Put him down!" Kip tugged at my arm.

"I saw him going at you with a weapon."

"What weapon?" he asked.

"Don't play dumb with me. I saw the metal in your hand."

Kip swooped down, then straightened, Harley's keys dangling from her outstretched hand.

"You mean this metal?"

I stared at it, frowning. "He was coming at you."

"He was walking toward me because he found these in the parking lot and wanted to know if they were mine."

"Why didn't he ask me if they were mine? He saw me when he first came in."

"You don't strike me as the kind of guy who would have a sparkly purple heart on your keychain," the man said.

I blinked, looking back at Kip, who held them up to me. The purple heart sparkled in the bright light of the station.

"Gave it to Harley for her last birthday. She hates it."

"Then why is it on her keychain?"

"Because I gave it to her."

I released the man.

"Thanks," he grumbled.

Kip pointed at him, giving me a penetrating stare. "Say you're sorry to the man you just assaulted."

"I'm sorry."

He held his hands up. "It's alright man. You're protecting your girl. I get it."

She put her hand on her hip, jutting it out. "I'm not his girl." She looked at me. "And the bitterness in your apology was a bit unnecessary." I gave her a blank stare. What did she expect of me? I was so confused. She sighed, rubbing her hand over her face. "Good enough."

The man walked off, grumbling something about just trying to do the right thing. I looked around and realized Harley hadn't come back. "Where did Harley go?"

Kip glanced out the window and pointed toward the car. "She's pumping the gas."

"Let's go."

The cashier handed me my bag and shot a glare at Kip as she took her change. Harley finished pumping and set the nozzle back in place as we got to the car.

"As soon as I saw your bodyguard over here go after that dude, I figured we were going to need as fast an escape from whatever ridiculousness he was going to cause."

She ducked into the car and Kip's lips curled up in a half smile as she started toward the other door. I reached out and took her by her wrist, pulling her back toward me. She looked surprised, her emerald eyes widening as she stopped a few inches from me.

"Are you sure you're all right?" I asked.

She nodded, innocent eyes staring up at me. "It was just keys. He wanted to get them back to us."

"I mean, other than that." A breeze picked up, fluttering a tendril of hair from the messy bun she'd spun a few hours into the trip. I brushed it away from her cheek, letting my fingers linger against her skin. Kip leaned her head subtly against my touch and my body moved closer to her. My breath deepened at the same moment hers caught in her chest. Her lips parted just enough for the tip of her tongue to slide across the bottom.

The sharp blaring of the car horn made her jump away from me. I looked through the window and saw Harley dangling over the front seat, leaning on the steering wheel. Kip glanced back at me for a brief second, then ducked her head and climbed into the backseat. I took a deep breath and got behind the wheel. The man I'd probably traumatized stepped out of the store and stopped when he saw me.

The stare was enough to shift my thoughts. Dealing with all of this was too much of a hassle. It would be easier to finish this and go back to the war.

I needed to kill Kip.

As soon as the thought went through my mind, I felt her reach over my shoulder to offer me the keys. Her hand brushed my palm, and everything tore inside me again.

CHAPTER 11

Kip

The look on Stryder's face had darkened in the seconds since we got into the car. There were a few breaths right before Harley scared the hell out of me when nothing had existed but him. The second he took my arm, he had all of me. I couldn't think of anything but his eyes staring deep into mine and the heat radiating between us. I thought he was feeling the same thing, but now it looked like he was ready to crush something with his bare hands.

That was not the type of reaction I'd really like to inspire in a man.

Out of the corner of my eye I noticed Harley staring at me. Her narrowed gaze was suspicious and I turned to it. "What?"

"You look strange. What's wrong?"

"Excessively pale skin and too bright hair that has about four personalities of its own? But, I mean... genetics."

"You know that's not what I meant."

"Actually, I don't ever really know with you. But in this

instance, probably, yeah. I'm just tired. This hasn't exactly been the most relaxing day off in the history of my career."

"I'm exhausted, too. We seriously have to stop."

"We have a full tank of gas," Stryder's deep voice filled the car, making me shiver.

Harley turned a slow glare towards him. "Does the amount of gas I just pumped into the car have some sort of direct correlation with our energy level? Or for that matter, our willingness to tolerate any more of your shit?"

"Yeah," I agreed, suddenly realizing that I didn't feel at all rested. "The last time I checked, it's the car that runs on the gas, not us. I, for one, got to the point where this road trip wasn't fun anymore about ten minutes before it started. We can't just keep driving forever. We have to stop and get some sleep at some point."

Harley nodded. "Unless fairies don't sleep."

"Fae." The correction surprised me when it came out of my mouth as much as it did Harley. She shot me a look, but I pretended not to notice. I thought I was firmly in the camp of thinking Stryder had misplaced his mind somewhere but might find it again before the end of this experience. Now it didn't seem so clear. His clear, intense eyes and the touch of his hand to my skin had changed something, and now I wasn't sure what I was supposed to think.

"We sleep. Not as much as you do, but we sleep."

"Then don't you think it would be a good idea to stop for the night?" I asked. "Especially if you are planning on continuing to bogart the steering wheel. You're the one who has been so adamant about not wanting to be easy to track. I dare say falling asleep and wrapping us around a pole will make it a hell of a lot easier for them to figure out where we are."

"Fine. When we find somewhere, we'll stop."

A few moments later a faded sign that looked like it had

been used for target practice on more than one occasion pointed us toward something called The Hemlock Inn.

"Look at that," Harley said. "Aren't we lucky?"

"Isn't hemlock poisonous?"

"I'm planning on sleeping, Kip, not licking the walls."

My nose wrinkled. "Do you frequently lick the walls of hotels?"

She winked. "Like you said, you never know with me."

"We're stopping." The severity in his voice was a step above a father ordering his children out of his recliner before a football game, but a little below Puritan executioner.

If it wasn't for the little red vacancy sign glowing in the front window of the office, the tiny motel would look abandoned. The parking lot in front of it was empty and there were no signs of life around any of the narrow blue doors positioned at tight intervals along the white building. It looked a little unnerving.

But Stryder didn't hesitate to park and, a few minutes later unlocked the door to the room Harley and I would share. She immediately tossed her bag on one of the beds and retreated into the bathroom. Within seconds, the sound of water rushing in the shower broke through the silence.

"I'm in the next room."

Stryder had scoured the room before letting me inside and then stood at the door and watched me as I milled around, trying to come up with things to do other than change in front of him.

"I know."

"The walls are probably thin, so if anything happens, just pound on it. I'll hear you."

"Thank you for the comforting image to go to bed with."

He hovered for a second longer, then stepped out and shut the door behind him. Expecting him to pop back in, I waited. When the door stayed closed, I stripped out of my clothes and dropped an oversized T-shirt down over my head. At least his unhinged packing had included a dip into my pajama drawer. The feeling of the fresh, clean cotton against my skin relaxed me and I crawled under the covers of the bed closest to the humming air conditioner. After several rolls and flops around in the bed, sleep was still totally eluding me. Harley hadn't gotten out of the shower yet and I resigned myself to the possibility she was just going to avoid reality by staying in there for the rest of the night.

Glancing at the clock to the side of the bed, I got the uncomfortable feeling that always came when I realized it wouldn't be long until it was time to get out of bed and get ready for work. Seconds later came the sinking realization that the work day wasn't coming for me. Even if Stryder snapped out of whatever was fueling his frantic need to run, there was no way we'd get back to Glendale in time for me to clock in for my shift at the bookshop.

I needed to let Mac know. It was late, but at least it would give him a heads up. The phone rang twice and Mac picked up. His voice sounded surprisingly awake.

"Did you just get up or have you not gone to bed yet?" I asked.

"A little of both."

"I don't know what that means."

"Is everything all right, Kip? You don't usually call at an hour like this."

I'd never called at an hour like this. "Actually, no. I wanted to let you know I'm not going to be able to get to the shop tomorrow for work."

"You aren't sick, are you?"

"No, not sick."

"I'm glad to hear that. What's going to be keeping you?" His voice held an edge of suspicion I hadn't expected.

It wasn't an out of line question, but still, I didn't have an answer prepared. Other than Harley, Mac was the person I trusted most. I talked to him when things were bothering me and tried to understand the advice he often cloaked in riddles. It made me want to share with him now, but coming up with what to say was the challenge.

I'm in a motel in the middle of nowhere with a man I barely know because he's sure someone is trying to kill me didn't flow off the tongue.

"Something unexpected came up. There was an emergency that took me out of town for a little while."

"Would it have something to do with the man at the park?"

I didn't see that coming. "Man at the park? Which man at the park?"

The one who grabbed me or the one who packed a bag for me before kidnapping me?

"A woman called the police, saying she witnessed two men fighting after one tried to snatch a redheaded woman."

So, both.

"That was me," I admitted.

"I figured as much. Not many others in Glendale who the only describing factor would be her hair. Are you all right? What happened?"

My eyes squeezed shut and I bit back the spiel of what was going on.

"Everything is all right. Stryder, the man who protected me, just thought it would be a good idea to get away for a bit while the whole thing died down. No big deal."

"Do you feel safe with him, Kip?"

My knees pulled up to my chest and I rested my forehead onto them. Talking to Mac was bringing up all the emotions I'd been trying to force down throughout this experience. It wasn't easy to feel them, but I was curious about what he would think.

"I think so. To be honest, I don't really know him. This all happened so fast and I'm not sure what to think about him or some of the things he's been telling me."

"Don't always think about just what you think is happening. Remember that words and actions can look one way but may conceal much more just beneath the surface. Just like in The Mist Realms from our story. You might think you are just walking through a gentle rain, but it is actually a sprite kissing you on the cheek."

I smiled. "Thank you, Mac."

"Get some rest, Kip. Keep in touch."

I'd already said goodnight and ended the call before it sank in just how strange and final his last comment really was. My head was almost on the pillow when the door swung open. Gasping, I bounced up into a sitting position and grabbed for the only thing within reach to protect myself.

It was a very good thing it was Stryder letting himself in the room because even as hard and flat as it was, the pillow probably wouldn't prove valuable as a weapon in a struggle for my life.

"What are you doing? How did you get in here?"

"The clerk gave us two keys. I kept one."

"Why?"

"To be able to come in and check on you."

"What happened to our wall communication plan?"

"That was for if something was happening."

I stared at him for a few seconds, waiting for his slip in logic to sink in. It didn't.

"So, shouldn't the fact that there was no pounding on the wall have told you there was nothing happening? Eliminating your need to storm in here and scare the pants off me?"

His eyes dropped to my bare legs and my cheeks burned at the acknowledgment that I wasn't, in fact, wearing any pants to be scared off. The look lingered longer than needed just to make his point and some of the intensity from the parking lot returned.

"I just wanted to check on you and make sure everything was fine."

"So what was the point of the wall communication plan to begin with?"

We were just talking in circles, so he seemed to decide to shift gears.

"What are you still doing awake? You said you were so tired, I thought you would have gone right to sleep when we got here."

"Me, too, but I was having trouble. My brain wouldn't quiet down, but I figured out it was because it still thought I needed to go to work. So I called Mac to let him know I'm not going to be there."

Stryder's face fell.

"You did what?"

"Called Mac. The owner of the bookshop? He was expecting me to be at work for my usual shift, but obviously that's not happening. There was no need to worry him, so I called and let him know."

"Get dressed." Scowling, he stomped over to the bathroom door and pounded his fist against it.

"What's going on?" I asked.

"Get out of the bathroom," he yelled at the bathroom door. "Get your stuff. Kip, put your clothes on. We have to leave."

CHAPTER 12

Stryder

Kip didn't budge and I took a frustrated step toward her. This woman was determined to get under my skin. "Put some clothes on," I certainly didn't want her leaving the motel like that, "and get your things."

Not bringing anything with me from Glendale had been an aggravating oversight, but now it seemed like a benefit. There would be no need for me to repack anything, shaving time off us getting back in the car and on the road.

"We just got here." She gave me a deadpan look.

The bathroom door opened and Harley walked out in pajamas, rubbing her wet hair with a towel. "What's going on?"

"We're leaving."

"No, we're not," Kip said. "We're going to bed. Harley and I already told you we're exhausted and done with this adventure of yours for the night."

I ground my teeth together. "We need to leave. Now."

"What the hell is going on?"

"Kip called her boss."

Harley looked at me and then at Kip. She threw her arms up in the air with an exaggerated look of shock. "How dare she? What kind of person would use readily available modern technology to keep in touch with a person who might worry when they don't show up to where they are supposed to be? Frankly, Kip, I'm surprised by you." She shook her head. "You think you know a person."

Her theatrical expression fell from her face and she walked over to the bed where she'd tossed her bag. Pushing it onto the floor, she stuffed herself defiantly beneath the covers.

"I'm serious." I growled out, so frustrated I wanted to tear my hair out. These girls were so irrational, it was a surprise we'd gotten this far. "We need to leave now."

"Why is me calling Mac such a big deal? I didn't tell him where we are, or anything about you or those guys. He knows about the attack at the park, but apparently everyone does."

"What do you mean?" Every instinct in me was suddenly on alert.

"Mac told me a woman called the police and reported the attack. She didn't call me by name, but he figured out it was me."

The urgency to leave just became vital. Another few seconds and I would have to toss Kip over my shoulder and haul her out to the car myself. Harley could stay there and live off the land for all I cared.

"You making that phone call exposed us. It drew attention to us and where we are. We aren't safe here anymore."

"It was one phone call and again, I didn't tell him anything about where we are. I didn't even mention the name of the motel, and he would have found it hilarious."

"You don't seem to understand the gravity of the situation we're facing."

"You see? I knew eventually you were going to catch on. No, I don't understand the gravity of the situation we're facing. It's probably pretty safe to say neither of us do, considering Harley has completely checked out of this conversation."

I looked over at the bed and saw Harley's head tucked under the pillow. One hand pressed it down to her ear to filter out our voices and the light coming from the lamp beside her. Stepping around the end of the bed brought me to within a few feet of Kip. She drew in a breath, but didn't move back.

"You are in incredible danger. You didn't reveal your location but they can track phone calls. There's no other way for me to explain that to you right now. Every second you keep standing here is making it more likely they are going to find you. We need to move on."

That seemed to make sense to her.

"Oh." Finally, she nodded. "Let me get dressed."

I stepped out of the room and pressed my back against the door. The rooms were along the side of the building, which meant the vantage point only allowed me to see part of the parking lot. My eyes swept back and forth, carefully taking in every detail as I tried to focus with all my senses. Finally, the door behind me opened and Kip joined me. A distinctly disgruntled Harley followed close behind. We moved quickly around toward where I'd parked Harley's car earlier. Within seconds, I noticed movement in the corner of the lot.

My head lifted sharply, my eyes darting around the space to search for what I'd sensed. There was nothing visible, but it felt like new sets of eyes were on us from all angles.

They were already here. I needed to break their tracking magic, immediately.

My hand grasped Kip's again and I moved her back into the shadows beside the building. Surprised, she stared up at me, blinking innocent, emerald eyes up at me that I wanted to drown in.

Before she could react, I pulled her up against me so that her body was pressed to my chest. My arms wrapped firmly around her, and my mouth on hers muffled her gasp.

Her lips were soft, so soft and sensual. I moaned, clasping my hand to the back of her neck to press her closer.

The kiss startled her, but she didn't resist or try to pull away from me. Heat radiated from her body and the taste of her lips was delicious and somehow familiar. She was like a magical drug, enticing and intoxicating. She was getting under my skin and filling the cavity of my chest. It was suffocating, the need to protect her, to touch her, to claim her.

The sensation of impending danger reached a harsh peak, then faded but I couldn't stop.

Everything in me said to ignore the feeling and keep my mind clear, but my desire was too strong. I couldn't stop. The tip of my tongue ventured closer toward her parted lips, seeking more of her warmth and taste. My teeth bit just enough into her bottom lip to draw out a slight whimper as my other hand slipped up under her shirt to the small of her back, just to feel her skin on my fingers. It burned through my fingers, traveling up my arm to my chest.

I stepped closer, trapping any space between us so that my whole body was pressed against hers and the mate bond snapped into place. I growled, my protective instincts raging inside. I would *never* let anyone hurt her.

Ever.

She was meant for me, and every inch of my body knew it, felt it. She was *made* for me.

I couldn't kill her, even if my whole realm was dying.

I physically couldn't.

I had to find a way to do both, save both her and my kingdom.

"What the hell are you two doing?" Harley's harsh voice filled my ears, snapping me out of it. "You dragged me out of bed just to make out in the shadows?"

Groaning, I forced myself to step away to snarl at Harley, angry she'd interrupted us. But Kip's eyes fluttered open and the sweet, innocent look on her face made my anger melt away. She was looking up at me, a thoughtful expression on her face, obviously waiting for an explanation. I suddenly remembered what we were doing. There wasn't time for explanations.

"Let's go." Grabbing her hand again, I took off across the parking lot, pulling her along with me. Harley fell into step behind us and we jumped into the car. In seconds we were speeding down the road away from the motel.

"What was that?" Kip said after a stretch of silence. "What just happened?"

"The Fae men from the Summer Court are close behind us and tracking you fast."

"So you thought that was the perfect time to call an impromptu game of tonsil hockey?" Harley snapped.

"Their tracking abilities are based on biological imprints and signals. The kiss disrupted those imprints and signals so the men lost track of her."

"Seriously?" Harley clearly didn't believe me.

I cleared my throat, swallowing down the desire to confess just how much I enjoyed the kiss and what it meant to me. "Hopefully it will continue to work enough to put some distance between us, but they aren't going to be held back for long."

"What are we supposed to do now?"

"Just keep going."

"Stryder, I need to understand what's going on."

Kip's voice shook slightly and I knew it was time. My decision had been made. The struggle between defending my kingdom and protecting my fated mate had kept my thoughts and emotions torn, but this had gone far enough. I felt calm and secure in what had to be done.

Both.

Kip would never die at my hands. There was no way I could bring myself to harm her in any way. But that didn't mean I was giving up on defeating the Summer Queen and ending the war. I had to find a way to protect her and also fulfill my duty to my people by bringing an end to the horror. The wizard prophecy that showed Kip saving the queen likely wasn't going to change. My advisers didn't have a precise, crystalline view of the future and everything that would happen. If they did, they would have been able to tell me what Kip was going to do to save her. But when an impression was strong enough to craft into a prophecy they shared with me, it was very rarely wrong.

It meant Kip was still destined to be a part of the war. Now it was up to me to make sure it was for the right side. Rather than destroying Kip before the Fae of the Summer Court could find her and present her to their queen, I would take her with me. Keeping her close would allow me to protect her, but also to prevent her from saving the queen. With that, I could change the course of what was ahead.

But that meant Kip needed to know more. She'd come this far with me. Even if she wouldn't yet admit to believing me, there was enough to stop her from just running away when she had the chance. There was more she needed to understand and there was no time left to hesitate.

CHAPTER 13

Kip

Every sound around me was muted except for the sound of my pounding heart. Heat buzzed over my skin, sparking and sizzling, lighting every pore on fire. Stryder and Harley were talking but I couldn't stop thinking about that kiss. He said it was to break their tracking, but his lips on mine and the heat of his body pressed against me felt like so much more.

Something I... something I couldn't quite put my finger on. But it seemed significant, in a strange way.

Like it bound us together, in only a way that he and I would ever have.

Goosebumps spilled over my skin at the thought and I shivered.

"The Land of the Sidhe is overseen by courts. The Dawn, Day, Twilight, and Night are in the north." The word 'night' snapped my attention back to him. "And the Fall, Winter, Spring, and Summer are in the south, with the Blood Court in the middle. Each of these is ruled by their monarchs. Some are more powerful and influential than others. The Summer Queen has long desired more power for herself. She disagreed with how many divisions there are and believed there should only be one monarch for the entirety of the world, and regents for smaller realms. As time has passed and people have disagreed with her, insisting on things staying the same, she has become more aggressive. It has erupted into war. Right now, we're the only thing between her forces invading the other Courts."

I tried to listen as carefully as I could but the way my heart was still pounding was distracting. I took in small sips, trying to calm it. Stryder continued on, telling us more about his people and the world he came from, with Harley pointedly expressing her doubts.

I had to agree with her. It all still seemed so strange, so outside of the sphere of what I thought could be possible.

But, he sounded sincere. These weren't the ramblings of someone disconnected from reality and he wasn't making it up as he went. He rattled off the details and described the land with the same confidence and smooth flow that I would have when talking about Glendale or the bookshop.

I waited for some sort of dramatic inflection or for him to seem like he was trying to get a rise out of me with something he was saying. That was always a tell when a person was weaving a complex lie or over-exaggerating something for the purpose of convincing someone else. There was always the subtle eyebrow raised or the measured pause. It was meant to underscore something or test the impact of a detail they'd carefully planned out. There was none of that in what Stryder was saying to me. He was as casual describing the hidden dangers of the murky Swamp Realm and the beautiful nurturers of the forest as I'd expect someone talking about the cornfield down the street. Everything was clear and straightforward. Just basic, simple reality.

But it wasn't just the way he was talking about his world. Something about what he was telling me struck a chord with me, but I couldn't quite put my finger on it. I listened silently, trying to figure out what it was that was making my skin prick and my heart pound. It was more than just the wonder of it all or trying to open myself to it. It felt oddly familiar.

Stryder detailed the war and the Summer Queen's reign of brutality with calm control. It wasn't that it didn't affect him. From the tension in his face and the ice in his eyes, I could tell he didn't want to put any emotion into it because it was causing him such deep pain. If he kept himself as distanced as he could, only telling the facts, he could get through it without being overcome.

"Why me?" I finally asked when Stryder had fallen silent for a few seconds. *Why did you really kiss me? Why touch me like you own me, look at me like I already belong to you?* These were the questions I really wanted to ask but didn't have the nerve. *And why do I feel something for you too, even though I barely know you. Something potent and pulsing, tugging me to you. Like I can't stop wanting to touch the fine lines of your face, listen to the deep tremor of your voice.*

"What do you mean?" His pointed question broke me out of my thoughts; I'd forgotten I'd even asked him anything. The skin of my face tinged red with my unspoken thoughts and I turned away, hoping he couldn't see it. I tried to focus. "What is it about me that is making all you Fae men crawl out of the woodwork to come for me? I never even knew the Fae world existed as an actual place. Why would I matter?"

"You are meant to play an important part in my world," Stryder started.

Before he could say anything else, the car made a strange sound and jolted. A few seconds later, it did it again. I gasped and grabbed the door.

"What was that?"

"I don't know. Something's going on."

"Harley, what's going on?" His brow furrowed. "Does your car do this often?"

She shook her head. "No. I've never heard it make that sound before."

It lurched again, this time accompanied by a sound like metal grinding and then a loud thud. The car shimmied and briefly stalled. I was relieved when it started back up.

"We are not going to be able to keep going like this. The car is going to break down and we can't have that happen when we're out here. I need to find somebody to look at it."

"Like who?" I asked.

"There was a sign a little while back for a town coming up. There has to be a mechanic in it. We'll just hope we can get that far."

My hand continued to grip the door tightly as we made our way down the gradually widening street. Relief washed over me when I saw buildings on either side of the road that eventually funneled together into a small downtown area. Just ahead of us an old gas station sign dangled from a larger sign promising honest and dedicated mechanic services. I didn't know how much I trusted the faded, tilted letters, but it was a mechanic and that was all that mattered.

The car seemed to get into the parking lot on little more than hope. It made a final gasping sound and then gave a loud clunk before falling dead just before Stryder parked. We got out of the car and pushed it the rest of the way into a parking space in front. Harley headed for the front door and a few minutes later I heard her shout a creative stream of profanities. Considering the time, those words were probably the first many people in that town were hearing for the day.

So much for a good first impression.

"What's wrong?"

"They aren't open," she said as she came back to the car. "Not for a while. There's a sign on the door. Apparently they like to go fishing in the morning."

We stood in the parking lot, staring around us as if at any second the mechanic was just going to appear to save us.

"Well, there's nothing we can do but wait," Stryder said. "Unless you know how to fix whatever's wrong with the car, we're not going anywhere else."

"So, that's just your decision? You say we're not going anywhere and we have to wait, and we just have to do it? You know, my car worked just fine until you started driving it."

"Like I said, unless you know how to fix whatever is wrong with the car, we don't have a choice."

"Isn't that convenient for you."

"Convenient for me? Do you honestly think any of this is *convenient*? You think I want to be doing the scenic tour of the abandoned corners of the human world?"

"Why are you doing it?" Harley snapped. "What are you getting out of this?"

"You wouldn't understand."

"How do you know that? You don't even know me."

"And yet you attached yourself to me."

"Don't flatter yourself. I didn't come to be with you. The only reason I'm here is Kip."

"She doesn't need you."

"Excuse me?"

I hadn't heard Harley so offended since someone asked if the purple streak she put through her hair one summer was a tribute to trolls.

"As long as I am near her, she doesn't need anyone else."

"You've known her for what... three days? I've spent my life with her. We went through hell together. Nothing is going to compare to that."

"I might not have spent the same amount of time with her as

you have, but that doesn't mean anything. Like I said... you don't understand."

Harley cocked her hip and rested her hand on it, staring at Stryder in disbelief. "You seriously think the world is yours to control, don't you? That everyone is just going to fall at your feet because of your fancy suit and the long hair?"

Stryder rolled his eyes so hard there was a touch-and-go moment where he might have just toppled himself right over in the parking lot. My stomach was starting to twist up. I hated listening to the two of them argue.

"If that were the case, there would be no war," Stryder said in a drawn-out voice like he had to explain it carefully to her.

"And that whole thing. Do you really believe that's true or are you trying to convince us so we'll go along with you? Because I'm genuinely trying to determine which is more disturbing... you living in the delusion that you are the King of Fairyland come to whisk Kip away and avenge your people, or the level of sociopathy required to tell that story without missing a beat in the belief it will get us under your control."

Stryder had started pacing, but Harley stood her ground. She watched him go back and forth, and it seemed like any second he might burst. I realized in a moment that could have been funny if we weren't in our current situation that it was the first time I'd ever wondered what it would look like when a fairy exploded.

Fae, I corrected myself, Fae. Not fairies.

"Again, you being here was never part of the plan."

"Right. So you just intended to manipulate Kip." Harley crossed her arms over her chest. Point made.

"I'm not manipulating anyone. There are far easier and less aggravating ways to impress a woman than going through this."

"Can the two of you just stop with the bickering for ten seconds? Seriously, this is ridiculous."

Both went silent when they looked at me, but Harley's arms

crossed over her chest and Stryder's flaring nostrils didn't give me a lot of confidence. The two had been at each other's throats almost since they met. To be fair, Stryder and I had also spent a good portion of our time together on less than friendly terms. But the ever-present heat between us and the feeling of that kiss were enough to take the edge off. There was some concern these two might legitimately attempt to take each other out at some point.

"We're not bickering. We're just having a conversation. I'm trying to figure this man out."

"Do you frequently accuse people you are trying to get to know of being a sociopath?"

"Do you frequently break the cars of people you don't know?"

"So now you're going to blame me for the car breaking down? This thing is probably older than you are."

I couldn't take it. My mind was already trying to grapple with too much to try to shoehorn playing referee into it as well. Even with the words flying between them, I didn't really think they hated each other. Right now, they were each other's outlet for the frustration and tension we were all feeling, which resulted in explosions between the two strong personalities. It also gave me the perfect opportunity to slip away from them and walk off. They were so caught up in their verbal tennis match, they didn't even notice me dip away and walk out of the parking lot.

Even though I felt bad about sneaking off without them, I needed some time to clear my head. My mind was like the moving truck the year Harley kicked her boyfriend out of her first apartment. So much stuff had been shoved into it, so fast, things started toppling over. It was all stuffed in my mind haphazardly. I didn't know what to think or to feel, or even if Stryder could be trusted. He had begun to sway me, and I wanted to believe him, but that meant believing in the danger chasing behind us. If I believed that, it would mean having to face the fear of it all.

Leaving Stryder and Harley gradually devolving into blaming each other for the mechanic not being there and the motel having uncomfortable sheets, I walked farther down the sidewalk. Around me, the town was going about its early morning routine and didn't seem to mind me sinking into it. The predicament made my mind wander to my father.

My father had always been the type of dad to leave little notes everywhere. All through my childhood after my parents adopted me, I'd find his encouraging words to me scrawled across a napkin tucked around the cupcake in my lunch or on a sticky note on the bathroom mirror. I even found them stashed in between the folds of my gown the day I graduated from college. One read:

Remember, on the road trip of life, it's not about the destination. It's about the journey.

A little cliché, but cute. It should have been followed up with: *Also remember, having roadside assistance doesn't mean calling me when you break down. Pieces of cars sometimes fall off.*

If it did, I could have shared that bit of wisdom with my best friend. Then my road trip of life wouldn't have featured a car giving the death rattle in the middle of nowhere and me wandering a tiny town with an honest-to-god stamp store while I'm stranded.

But it didn't. So, I couldn't.

The buildings packed tightly on either side of the narrow main street were enough to keep me occupied while my brain went to work untangling the knot of all that had happened. There was plenty to explore, starting with the stamp store. The nostalgia and novelty alone were enough to draw me inside. After a half hour spent listening to a man who seemed mere moments away from aging into dust wax poetic about the price of stamps and how they were no longer sincere, I'd had enough.

Slipping out with a wave of the commemorative stamp I'd been talked into buying, I continued on. The next few shops didn't hold much interest or were still closed. I was contemplating a visit to the lunch counter for a root beer float when a sound like a gust of wind startled me. The sound was distinct enough that I expected to feel coolness on my skin, but the air around me was completely still. None of the few people going about their lives along the street acted like they'd heard it and after a moment I made my way into the soda shop.

The waitress didn't seem to approve of my decision to greet the morning with ice cream and soda, but I was an adult and sticking to my guns. Perching on a stool by the window as I sipped the float gave me a view of the stores across the street.

"What's that?" I asked a passing waitress, pointing at a shop that caught my eye.

"Sue's Bookshop," she told me. "Woman's got more books than she's got good sense. Her lack of floor space is testament to that. Interesting place, though, if you're looking for something to read."

A bookstore. That was exactly what I needed; something to make me feel a little more at home. My straw made a loud sucking sound as it gathered the last creamy bits of the float and I handed the glass to the waitress along with some folded-up cash.

"Thank you," I said.

Homesickness and intrigue brought me out of the diner and across the street toward the bookshop. It looked older than the buildings on either side, like the rest of the town had built up around it, and the inside looked so dark through the front window I wasn't sure it was open, but a tug on the door easily opened it. Bells jangled overhead just like at Mac's, but they didn't elicit a greeting from anyone inside. My eyes swept around for a few seconds before I stepped inside.

"Hello?" My voice sounded impossibly loud moving through

the shadowy back corners. "Wow," I murmured, taking in the surroundings. "Girl wasn't kidding."

There must be something in the small independent bookshop owner's credo that dictates the sheer number of books necessary for a shop to be legitimate. This space looked like a shrunken-down version of Mac's shop. Books filled virtually every inch of the space, including large swathes of the mauve carpet. Some of the titles were brand new while other fabric-bound volumes gathered layers of dust on layers of dust.

Empty areas peeking up from the carpet created openings to several narrow, weaving paths that led to the row of shelves. The stacks of books on the floor concealed where each path really ended up, meaning whichever one I chose held my literary fate.

"This must be what it's like for our customers when they first show up," I murmured, not remembering my first visit to my beloved shop. "We're just going to consider this a sensitivity training seminar."

The nearest path brought me to an aisle flanked by shelves stuffed solid with pulpy vintage paperbacks and I pried one out of place. My fingertips had just touched the dry, textured pages when the jingling bells announced I had company.

Pausing, I listened to hear the greeting no one offered me. When it didn't come, I offered it.

"Hello." Silence. "People sure are friendly around here."

The first sentences of the book didn't snare my attention, so back to the shelf it went. I turned around to choose another path and my heart jumped into my throat. A dark-eyed man stood only a few feet from me. He didn't look familiar, but an uncomfortable sensation crept along my skin when he looked at me. I knew I needed to get back to Stryder. The door was only a few steps away, but in an instant the man closed the space between us, blocking my way.

CHAPTER 14

Stryder

A strange feeling in my gut told me that it wasn't a coincidence that Harley's car had broken down but I didn't want to alarm them, so I said nothing about it. The crunch of feet on gravel was an optimistic sign the mechanic had finished his fishing for the day and arrived at the shop. When I turned around, greeting him became the last thing on my mind.

"Where's Kip?"

"What?" Harley asked. "What do you mean where's Kip?"

"I mean, where is she? She's not here."

Some of the tightness fell from Harley's face as she looked around and realized Kip was no longer where she'd been.

"She was right here. She was standing with us."

"When was the last time you saw her?"

Harley shook her head. "I don't even know."

Worry surged up from my chest. We'd been standing here arguing just for the sake of getting out our aggression and at some point Kip had disappeared. A second later my feet pounded on the sidewalk, carrying me further into the town. I focused intently on the feeling in my chest that had formed when I first saw Kip. Now that the painful ache as I tortured myself over my choices were gone, the warmth in my chest was even stronger. It pulled me to her.

The concept of Kip being my fated mate was still hard for me to fully understand. These types of connections were once common among my kind. It wasn't unusual for people to discover a fated mate and spend their lives with them. Those days had long since passed. Now it's rare for fated mates to exist at all, much less for them to find each other and have the chance to be together. Feeling this attachment to her was strange and new and being able to use it was unfamiliar. But I couldn't let that stop me. I had to do whatever I could to find her.

That feeling guided me along the sidewalk and when I saw the tiny bookshop nestled between the other stores, I knew that's where she was. It brought me across the street without bothering to look and I yanked the door open.

Inside, Kip ran across the shop and a man chased after her. The sight of him reaching out and grabbing onto her made my vision go red. Kip clutched desperately onto the counter, her fingertips clinging to the edge to resist the dark figure trying to drag her away.

"Let go of her!" I roared, rushing toward them.

Snatching the back of his cloak, I yanked him back hard. His arm slipped away from Kip and she fell to the floor. She scrambled away as I pulled the man toward me and shoved his hood away. His face was immediately familiar, and my stomach turned at the memories of the battlefield it brought into my mind.

"Give up, Stryder," Xavier growled, his eyes wild. "The queen's rule is unbreakable. You will never control The Land of Sidhe."

"Queen Ajeka is a false ruler. She has no claim to the Sidhe and I will destroy her."

It was the first time I'd said the Summer Queen's name since the start of the war, and it burned like acid on my tongue.

Xavier's head fell back as he let out a cruel, twisted laugh. The smash of my knuckles into his mouth cut off the sound, letting me hear the desperate whimper coming from the front of the shop. I looked to the side and saw Kip throwing her weight against the door, then yanking on it frantically.

"It won't open," she cried. "I can't get out."

I shook Xavier.

"Open the door," I demanded.

The queen's minion spit blood but said nothing. To either side, concealed in the shadows, the sound of rushing air announced the arrival of more Fae. Two more cloaked figures stepped into the hazy light trickling down from the tinted glass fixtures in the ceiling. One lifted his hand sharply toward the front, and the glass of the windows and door shattered. Kip screamed as the bits of glass rained down on her. In the same instant, impenetrable walls replaced the glass. From the outside, the shop would look the same, the magic he used concealing what he'd done from anyone who walked by.

"Get the girl," Xavier commanded.

I buried my knee in his stomach, dropping him to the ground, and stomped down to ensure he wouldn't be moving for a while. Kip clawed at the wall, looking back over her shoulder. A primal, protective urge rushed up inside me when I saw the terror in her eyes. I stepped toward her, but before I could get there, the second cloaked figure reached out one hand and swept it in front of his body. The force of the gesture took hold of Kip and sent her flying across the shop. Her back crashed into one of the shelves and she slid to the floor, books tumbling down over her.

I launched at the man, burying my shoulder in his stomach to bring him to the floor. My fists pummeled his face until the hood fell away and I could see him clearly. Climbing to my feet,

I reached down, entangling a band of magic around his throat so he lifted up over my head.

"Leave her alone," I commanded.

My other hand pushed the third man back as I lifted the second slightly higher. Tossing him to the ground several feet away, I rushed toward where Kip lay. She groaned as I slipped one arm under her shoulders and tenderly brushed the strands of hair away from her face.

"Are you all right?" I said softly. "Kip? Look at me."

Long lashes fluttered up and she met my eyes.

"I'm all right."

"Good." I ran my fingertips along the line of her jaw. The warmth rushed through me and a primal urge to put myself between her and any possible danger took over. I scooped her up into my arms to carry her to the back of the shop, where I lowered her to the floor again. "Stay here. When you hear me call for you, don't wait."

She nodded and I darted back to the front of the store. Two of the servants were on their feet again. I couldn't let them get to Kip and bring her back to Queen Ajeka. A shudder of disgust went through me. I hated even thinking her name. Running toward the man I knew as Blaine, one of the queen's youngest but most fervent of servants, I jumped into the air and planted my foot into his face. My wings strained where I'd bound them down before coming to the human world, but I couldn't open them. It was risky enough to use the magic we had. I had to rely as much as I could on my strength alone. I knew my desire to protect Kip and get her away from these men would give me all I needed.

Blaine and I fell to the ground and I didn't hesitate to stand and lunge at the third man. I didn't recognize him, but he glared at me with the same bloodthirsty hatred as the others. His hand lifted and I grabbed hold of it, shocking him with the sudden, unexpected motion. The bone of his wrist cracked as my hand twisted his arm away from me and I ran forward to force him back. Slamming him against the corner of a heavy shelf brought him to his knees and I smashed my fist up under his jaw to render him unconscious. I turned back to Blaine. His eyes glowed and the air shimmered like trapped heat as he seemed to dissolve away. It wouldn't be for long. The feverishly loyal man wouldn't retreat. He was going for others, which meant we only had a little time to get out.

"Kip!"

She came running and jumped into my outstretched arms. Surprised, I pulled her close. It was an unexpected gesture, but she felt natural and comfortable in my arms. My fingers traced lightly through the wild red curls that were so very her, then along the side of her neck. I could feel her pulse there, racing just beneath the surface of her delicate, translucent skin. An irresistible urge made me dip my head and brush my lips across the rhythm. The life rushing through her made me feel at once stronger and weaker.

Her breath shuddered with uncertainty as she stepped back from me. "I just wanted a few minutes to get my head clear and I found this place. It reminded me of back home and I came in…"

"It's fine," I soothed. "As long as you're alright."

"I am. Probably be sore tomorrow, but I'm alright."

"I don't think I am."

We looked in the direction of the voice and saw Harley crawling out from behind a large overstuffed armchair several feet from the door.

"Harley!" Kip gasped. "When did you get here?"

"I followed Stryder and got inside right after he did. Just in time for all living hell to break loose. What just happened?"

"Those were the servants of the Summer Queen. They found us."

"Fantastic. So now what are we supposed to do? I thought

this messed up *Thelma and Louise* situation was to keep us away from them," Kip said.

"They sent their best trackers. It was only going to keep them at bay for so long. That fight pushed them back and bought us some time. We just have to keep going."

CHAPTER 15

Kip

Harley rushed over to us as Stryder led me to where the door used to be. The solid wall in front of us spiked my anxiety. I had never been claustrophobic, but it felt like the already tiny shop was closing in on me. Not being able to see through the windows or simply open the door and walk outside made it seem like every breath was using up the air and we were starting to suffocate.

"You know those fruit baskets Lidia makes down at her shop?" I asked, glancing over at Harley. "She uses that heat gun that looks like a big hair dryer to shrink the plastic up against them."

Harley nodded.

"Yeah. It's like that, this whole place."

She made a slurping sound and pulled her hands in close to her like she was demonstrating being sucked in by the shrink wrap. She was feeling the same closed-in anxiety.

"Do you know how to get out?" I asked Stryder. "Maybe we can break something."

"They may be able to close us in, but I can open it back up."

He flattened his palm against the barrier. The area around his hand glowed briefly before the wall cracked and crumbled away. He dug through the broken pieces to create an open space and stepped through. I took his outstretched hand to let him help me climb out. The touch was electrifying. How I felt every time his skin met mine was intense, heightening all my senses, but I couldn't get enough of it. The more I felt the connection between us building, the more I wanted to explore it.

As soon as we were back on the sidewalk, I turned to look at the shop. There was nothing different about it. It looked like we had just walked back out through the door and into the small town again.

"Well, that was very dramatic," Harley said. "I liked the whole Terminator thing you had going on there. But why am I seeing a door? Why can't I see the wall we just had to smash our way through?"

"It's an illusion. You don't want the humans around here to know anything strange is happening, so they concealed their magic as soon as we were inside. From the outside, the shop looks no different than it did so no one will suspect anything."

"Except for the poor owner," I pointed out. "The waitress across the street told me this place is owned by a woman named Sue. From the looks of it, she's not just some casual bookstore owner. She loves this place and the books in it. What's going to happen when she shows up later to open up? Is she going to be able to open the door and go inside or is she going to try and end up climbing through the wall? How is she going to feel when she sees the destruction in there?"

"Something tells me she's not going to mind as much as you think she would."

"What does that mean?"

Stryder looked back and forth down the sidewalk to make sure no one was close enough to hear us.

"That shop is owned by a Fae."

He started walking, but the revelation shocked me so much I didn't fall into step behind him. He stopped and turned around to stare expectantly at me.

"How do you know that?" I asked.

"There are ways to tell. Not many of my kind live in the human world, but when they do, they maintain elements of themselves we can recognize. Some of the signs aren't voluntary. They're just a part of them they aren't able to change even outside of their own world. But there are others they do on purpose to signal others."

"They hang up the Fae shingle."

"Essentially. It makes it so if there is a time when others come their way, they can more easily recognize one another and be able to interact comfortably. It's a sign of safety. Both for Fae wanting a friendly face in the human world, and so those who might be prone to treat humans less than kindly will know to bring their attention elsewhere."

"That's a good ambassador program you have set up."

"It's reality. Most in my world are kind and happy to coexist with many other species, including humans. But just like in the human world, there are some who see anyone being different as an invitation for retaliation or mistreatment. Making sure their true identity is obvious to those who know what to look for is just a way to protect themselves and others."

We started quickly down the sidewalk in the direction of the garage.

"But aren't you able to recognize your own kind already?" I asked.

"Most of the time it's fairly easy. Sometimes it might be more ambiguous."

"How can you tell?" Harley asked. "You look just like humans."

"To you. That's something we do on purpose. When we

come into the human world, we don't exactly want to advertise our existence. We use glamours to conceal certain features and create an appearance that is easier for the humans who see us to accept."

"What do you mean certain features? Like if you weren't using the 'glamour' things we would be able to see you all tiny and sparkly? Or is this more of a goblin situation?"

Stryder's eyes slid over to Harley with an expression that said he couldn't tell if she was being purposely offensive or just oblivious. His eyebrow arched, his voice deep and gruff. "Tiny and sparkly?"

"They aren't tiny and sparkly," I told her.

I remembered my birthday and the first time I noticed the men paying attention to me. Knowing now who and what they were, the strange flickers I thought I'd noticed meant more. What I thought was just my eyes playing tricks on me or the odd attention messing with my head was actually me seeing through cracks in their glamours.

"You could see them," Stryder said.

It wasn't a question but an acknowledgement, a statement of something he already suspected.

"I think so. They first started showing up at the bookshop on my birthday. They just looked like normal guys, but every now and then it would be like they would... change. It's hard to explain. They didn't look the same. It was like if I caught them at just the right angle or out of the corner of my eye, they looked bigger and more frightening."

"You were seeing their true form."

"But if they came here to kidnap Kip, why would they want to look less intimidating?" Harley asked. "Wouldn't they want to be able to scare her?"

"Not necessarily. Remember, they want to blend in with the humans. Even when they are trying to be as appealing as they can be, they still don't want anyone to think they are anything but human. Coming in fully visible in their true form would terrify people. They hoped to come in, sweep her off her feet, and get back smoothly. That wouldn't happen in a town of suspicious humans."

"Why could I see them? If that's part of their magic and something they're used to doing, how could I get past it?"

"I don't know. Some Fae are more skilled at glamours than others. Some are so accustomed to their glamours they are in place at all times and can be undetectable, even to other Fae. Some don't really have the hang of it. The prophecy that brought the Fae men here to find you specified your importance would really begin on your twenty-first birthday. All I can think is it has something to do with that."

I wanted Stryder to be more confident. This was all still so new and overwhelming, and he was my only touchpoint. Him not knowing all that was happening made me feel even more like I was dangling out on a limb somewhere.

"Did you know there was a Fae here when we got to this town?" I asked.

"No, but it's not unheard of. There are some scattered around. But it might work to our advantage."

He didn't elaborate and I didn't have a chance to ask. The sight of the car still up in the air when we got to the shop didn't make the situation feel any more hopeful. Stryder jogged up to it and ducked his head down to talk to the mechanic. His head was shaking as he came back toward us.

"It's not ready. The guy said it might be a few more hours. He's having a hard time fixing it, other things keep breaking."

"That sounds very suspicious." Harley's hands were pressed to her chest, a frown on her face. "And very expensive."

"A few more *hours*? What are we supposed to do?" I asked.

"I don't know, but we can't just hang around here waiting for those guys to show back up," Harley said.

"No, we can't. We need to get going," Stryder agreed.

"Do you know where we are going next?" she asked.

"Yes," Stryder said. "The Fae woman owning a shop here and the men getting here so fast means there is a portal back to my world close by. I'll be able to locate it when we're on our way."

There was the advantage.

Harley's eyes swept around the parking lot and she took a step in closer to us. "Good. Now, do either of you have strong feelings about grand theft auto?"

What? I jolted, then raised my hand. "Me. I do. I have *very* strong feelings about it."

"Okay. How about borrowing a car for a short period and then leaving it somewhere nice and conspicuous so the police can find it and return it to its rightful owner?" I stared at her in surprise, looking from her to Stryder, who didn't seem to be all that offended. I sighed, running my hand over my face.

What the hell. We'd come this far. Why not sprinkle a little felony into the mix?

"How are you going to do that?" Stryder asked.

"Some skills compliments of the shadier parts of my life." She looked to me for approval. "Kip?" I shrugged. "Good enough. Start walking out of the town."

I didn't hesitate. Stryder caught up with me a few steps later.

"That's ominous," he said.

"Of everything that's been going on for the last couple days, this is what's going to stand out to you?"

We walked in silence for a moment before he looked at me again.

"You need to come to the Land of Sidhe with me. When we get to the portal, you need to come through."

"I thought we were trying to keep me *away* from the other Fae."

"There's a prophecy about you, Kip." He grabbed my arm, stilling me, and a tingle shot through it. His gaze bore into me, his face serious. "You are going to play a critical role in the war. I *need* you to come with me and save my people."

I had a strange feeling that there was something deeper going on. There was something in the way his gaze bore into me, his hand clasped to me tight, a hesitation in his voice after he said the word 'need'. Almost as if he'd wanted to say something else.

And then the rest of that sentence sunk it. Save his people?

Suddenly, a burgundy Oldsmobile pulled up beside us and the window rolled down. "Hop in," Harley said. "Make it fast. The mechanic was trying to scramble out from under my car when I drove away."

CHAPTER 16

Kip

Stryder's words struck me so hard I couldn't figure out how to respond to him. I stood there staring at Harley for long enough her face dropped.

"What's wrong? What's going on?"

"Nothing," Stryder said, taking me by the arm and guiding me through the car door.

The dark gray leather seats felt hot under my hand and I could only imagine what it must be like to try to travel in something like this during the middle of summer. All it would take was one ill-timed traffic jam and you'd be commiserating with those loaves of bread slapped up on the sides of ovens. He took the seat beside me. It felt like he was staying as close to me as he could so the second I made my decision, he would be able to act on it.

"Where are we headed?" Harley asked, glancing in the rearview mirror.

"Just keep going. I'll tell you when to turn."

"What do you mean I'm important to the war?" I asked.

"Important to the war? What are you talking about? What happened in the two minutes I was gone?" Harley turned around in the driver's seat and I pointed to the windshield.

"This is not a simulation, Harley. You are in control of this motor vehicle and I'd appreciate it if you catch up with that. There's enough shit going on in my life right now. I don't want to have gone through all of it only to end up as an unidentifiable streak across the highway."

Grumbling, she turned back around. Her confused eyes focused on us in the rearview mirror again. "Whatever you said to her, it probably could have waited until we found us some coffee."

"There aren't enough beans in all of Columbia to help me deal with this morning," I grouched.

"My world is depending on you," Stryder said. "I know you don't understand that, and that's frustrating, but you're going to have to trust me."

"Seriously?" Irritation sparked in my chest. I turned around sharply in my seat and glared at him. "You know, you keep saying that. It's like every other thing out of your mouth. I just have to trust you. Well, the thing is, you haven't really done a whole lot to inspire that trust in me. You did just save my ass in that bookshop, and I really appreciate it, but that's a big reciprocation you're asking me for."

He looked down and his tongue slipped across his lips. It immediately reminded me of that one intense kiss, making my irritation transform into a deep burning, longing. Despite everything, I still felt so drawn to him. It was taking everything in me not to just slide across the sticky leather bench and curl up against him. He was the one causing all the confusion and upheaval in my mind, but he was also the only one I wanted to comfort me.

This was not what I had imagined twenty-one looking like.

"What are you talking about?" Harley asked.

Stryder's deep blue eyes slid over to me. He spoke to me like I was the only person in existence. Not just the only other person in the seat or in the car, but the only person who he ever meant to hear his voice.

"My world is dying. My people are being slaughtered or dragged away to be held in dungeons and forced into slavery. As King of the Blood Court, I am who everyone is looking to to save them. But it's not just me, Kip. They are entrusted into my hands, but you are the one who will decide what happens to them."

"You still haven't told me what that means."

"Because I don't know for sure."

"Well, that is super encouraging. Let me just swear my allegiance and devote my future to a complete stranger with absolutely no plan who has no idea why I matter."

"Is that what I am to you?" His voice was lower, rough, and vibrated right through me.

"What?" The question took me off guard and made my heart speed up.

"Is that what I am to you? A complete stranger?"

My breath caught in my throat. *Of course* he was. And yet, he wasn't. Something deep and primal inside me responded to him. Something comforting and familiar. "No," I whispered back, barely able to speak.

His hand slid across the seat toward me, his fingertips grazing mine. Suddenly the heat didn't feel like it was just coming from the leather.

"I'm asking for you to believe me."

It was an overwhelming decision. I wanted to answer him, to say anything, but the words wouldn't happen. Everything was so confusing and yet, I wanted to believe him, to trust him. Sounds formed in my throat, an attempt to answer him, but got lost somewhere between there and actually coming out. Finally,

Harley took a sharp turn, startling me out of the trap of thoughts that held me.

"We're stopping," she said.

"I told you I would tell you where to go."

"And you haven't said shit, so I took over my own navigating."

"Sisters are doing it for themselves," I said.

"That's right." Harley nodded. "I'm exhausted. You might not need much sleep, but I at least need some. In the last day we've gotten only a couple hours smashed up in the back seat of a compact car. That is not exactly the restorative rest this whole situation is going to require. So we're stopping."

"Where?"

"I noticed a sign for another hotel a couple miles this way. The two of you can continue to stare meaningfully at each other there. But if you ask me, I think Kip should at least get some shut eye before the end of the world comes for her."

"You can pull over and get out if you don't want to keep going. This isn't about you."

Stryder's face darkened and I took his hand. The touch brought his seething glare away from Harley and a more determined look back to me. His Adam's apple bobbed.

"Give us some time. We need to wrap our brains around it."

His head dipped in what I decided to take as an affirming nod. "Should I stop?" she asked.

I nodded but didn't look away from Stryder's face. "It's time for a shower and some sleep."

Harley let out something that sounded like a little *yay* under her breath and turned in to a gravel parking lot marked with an aging white hotel sign. It was more welcoming than the last place, but it probably wouldn't have mattered to me if it wasn't. She could have chosen a half-rusted camper in the middle of a campground and as long as there was something resembling a shower and a bed, I'd take it.

We went through the same process of checking in and having Stryder scan our room before letting us inside. When he finally determined it was safe, he stepped to the door.

"I'll stand guard. If you need me, I'll be right here."

"Should I pound on the wall?"

His serious expression melted the smile that came to my lips. "Just scream."

"That man needs to work on his interpersonal skills," Harley said when I closed the door behind me.

"Yeah."

I rifled through my bag to choose fresh clothes but couldn't focus enough to get past a pair of socks.

"Or does he?" The smirk on her face reflected in her voice. "Is he just using up all those particular skills with you and doesn't have any left for me?"

"What's that supposed to mean?"

"Um, that kiss?"

"You also heard why it happened. He was just trying to keep those men from being able to track me."

She shook her head. "I don't think so. That was scorching hot! I thought you two were going to melt into the concrete."

I scoffed, not yet ready to tell her how I really felt. How it had torn out my insides, making me raw, inside and out. How it had changed nothing, and yet everything all at once. I finally managed to yank out the right combination of clothing to cover all the essential areas of my body and shot her a glare.

"I need a shower." I padded across the room and closed the bathroom door behind me, muffling out whatever Harley said after that. After waiting for the shower to heat, I stepped under the stream and turned my face into it. The pressure was not what I hoped for at the end of the last two days. My muscles needed to be tenderized with a merciless pulse setting. This felt like kittens licking me into submission. But it was hot and a whole teeny bottle of body wash cut through the grime. The whole teeny bottle of shampoo made me feel like a person again. Harley would just have to settle for the bar by the sink.

Even with the fresh smell of hotel amenity soap coming up from my skin, I wasn't ready to get out of the shower. Standing in the hot water made me feel like I could think without expectant eyes on me. This only lasted a few moments before the door opened and Harley came in.

"So?"

"So, what? What are you doing, Harley?"

"You're taking too long so I decided to come in here to finish our conversation."

"The conversation we finished out there?"

"If it was finished out there, I wouldn't be in here trying to finish it. Now, spill. What's actually going on?"

"What do you think about all this? About everything Stryder's been saying?"

"That's not exactly an answer to my question, but I'll bite." She paused, thinking, then sighed. Big. "Honestly, I have no idea what to think. It sounded crazy as hell when he started down that fairy path."

"Fae."

"Whatever. I'm never going to get used to having a politically correct title for things I didn't know were real."

"Well, I might have to get used to it. He wants me to go back there with him."

"Excuse me? Girl, get out of the shower." Harley's hand shoved a towel through the side of the curtain to me and I turned off the water before wrapping it around myself. Her eyes were wide and her mouth open when I stepped out.

"He wants me to go back with him," I said as I got dressed. "That's what he was telling me when you pulled up in that stolen car."

"Borrowed. Why would he want you to go back there?

Wasn't the point of this whole messed-up holiday road trip about keeping you away from there?"

"That was my thought, but apparently he just doesn't want me to go there with those guys." We walked out of the bathroom and the cooler air sent a chill along my steamed skin. I bounced down on the end of the bed. "He said he is holding his world in his hands, but I'm the one who will determine what happens in the war."

"What is that supposed to mean?"

"I have no idea, but it scares me. How could I possibly be so important to a war I didn't know was happening in a place that shouldn't really exist? But when I look at him..." I shook my head. "He's already put us through so much. I just don't know what I'm supposed to do."

CHAPTER 17

Stryder

I intended to stand directly outside the door to Kip's hotel room for as long as she needed but the stress was getting to me. Just standing here, doing nothing, made me restless and out of control. Kip's response was the turning point in all of this, and I didn't expect to have to wait for it. She should have just trusted me, just come with me when I told her how important it was. Her resistance baffled me.

Didn't she understand what was on the line?

Even now, it was my intense need to protect her that had me pacing back and forth along the narrow strip of concrete in front of the door.

It felt like hours since I'd heard the lock flip into place on the other side of the door. The faint sound of the shower and muffled voices let me know the women inside were safe for a time. But then it fell silent; they were asleep. I had to remind myself that's why we were here in the first place. Kip and Harley were worn down and needed to rest. Not being able to hear them anymore was a good thing.

Except that it meant I had no way to monitor Kip. It probably would've been easier at night. The sun still being high overhead made me feel more on edge.

When I first came to the human world it was with one purpose in mind. The thought of killing her had barely affected me until the moment I saw her.

With that same intense focus I could take her and force her to come with me. There was no actual need to give her the time she'd asked for, but I knew I could never force her to come with me.

To everyone else she was a human woman with an inexplicable link to my world.

She was so much more to me. Kip was created for me and as my mate, she was my responsibility, even above everything else.

Keeping Kip safe was more than just rescuing her from Keilen or fighting the men in the bookshop. That ensured she stayed physically safe and alive. My protectiveness of her went beyond that. I wanted her to feel safe. That meant giving her back some of her sense of control and allowing her to try to come to terms with the choice ahead of her. But it also meant not telling her everything as I couldn't bring myself to put more on her. Now wasn't the time to reveal the powerful link between us. I could see it when she looked at me, feel the connection strengthening. Telling her any more would only make this entire situation harder and more confusing.

The priority now was getting her to the Land of Sidhe. Once she was in my realm, she would be away from immediate danger of the Queen's men. I could better protect her and reveal more as the time came.

The other problems hovering in the back of my mind would just have to be dealt with later.

Only one of them being my men. It was hard to know what to expect when I got back there with Kip. Someone might push back against me. I knew even among the most loyal I'd left behind there would be those who resented my choice. There'd been no doubt in the need to fulfil my mission the morning I walked away from them. In their minds, as soon as I accepted the responsibility, Kip was as good as dead. The threat she represented was gone. The shift in that reality and the changes it would require might be hard on them.

I frowned, the need to protect her overwhelming all else.

The men had one choice.

They stood with me, and extend that loyalty to her, or they were against us.

I would accept nothing less.

A sound like a gust of wind and a flicker of movement across the parking lot made my muscles tense. I positioned myself back in front of the door and squared off against the hooded impending figure. Whoever it was, he was one of my kind. That sound indicated rare magic. It accompanied Fae transporting themselves across the divide between the human and Fae worlds without the regulation of a portal. Very few were capable of using it and traveling that way had become increasingly treacherous during the war.

My hand ached for my broadsword. Standing there with only a flimsy hotel door behind me to protect Kip, I hated being unarmed. The figure got closer and I was ready to surge forward to stop him before he got to me, but he spoke.

"Stryder!"

The man removed his hood, revealing his face.

I blinked in surprise. "Roane, what are you doing here?"

My best friend rushed up to me with urgency and terror in his eyes. I had never seen him look like that. A warrior and a fierce defender of what he believed, Roane had always shown quiet strength and determination in the face of danger. It was he who'd made me continue to commiserate with Harley, even when she pushed me into the edge of my tolerance. Like her,

Roane struggled with his identity and how his earliest years had shaped him.

Though raised alongside me, he wasn't of the Blood Court. He was originally a knight from the Night Court but had been taken from there when he was still very young. His entire kingdom was wiped out, leaving Roane without parents or anyone else in the Night Court to rely on. The life he had been given in the Blood Court had been good, but it didn't change what was inside him.

The longing to return home, to serve the king and queen of the court of his birth.

"You have to get back." His voice was urgent.

"It won't be long," I told him. "I'll be on my way soon."

"Soon isn't good enough, Stryder. You need to get back to our world immediately. The Blood Court is falling."

My stomach fell. "What's happening?"

"There's been tremendous danger in only the short time you've been away. The Summer Queen knows you're gone and has taken advantage of the vulnerability of the realms. She acted fast and sent in the fiercest armies I've seen come from her court. We thought we understood her tactics and were prepared for what was coming next, but she changed it. All along she crafted her methods and let us believe we knew what her next steps were. We never did. Without you, there isn't a chance. The Blood Court will be destroyed."

"We'll get to the portal as fast as we can."

"We don't need to use the portal. I can transport you with me."

"No. It isn't just me," I told him.

"I don't understand. You came here alone." He stared back at me in confusion.

I grit my teeth, determinedly. "Yes. But I'm going back with her."

"What do you mean?" Roane put his hand on my shoulder.

"Kip is coming back with us." My fist pounding on the door sounded like gunshots through the still afternoon. A few seconds' pause brought no response, so I pounded again.

"She's alive?"

He nearly hissed the words and I whipped around to face him. The burning, primal protectiveness nearly lashed out against Roane, but I forced it down. He didn't know what had happened. Just like the others, he expected me to have finished what I came here to do and be ready to go back.

"Yes, and she is going to stay alive."

"I don't understand, Stryder. What's going on?"

"There's no time to explain it right now, but instead of killing her, I've decided to bring her with us." I grasped his arm to give him a determined gaze. "This is important, Roane."

He gave me an intense stare, then, swallowing hard, nodded. He would stand with me, as I'd hoped.

"She doesn't know about the prophecy or why the wizards sent me, yet. So be careful with your words." I turned back to the door and pounded on it again. The sound finally got through to the sleeping women and footsteps stumbled toward the door. I stormed into the room, facing Kip. Sleep had messed her hair and her eyes were barely open.

And yet, she looked as beautiful as that first night in the bar, if not more. Her lips were plump and so delectably bitable. Her nightgown thin, unveiling the outline of her sexy form. The top buttons of it were undone, revealing the tender swell of her breasts.

I hadn't been able to keep my eyes off her that night but now… now she was sleep tossed and incredibly sensual. It was a reminder that she'd just been in bed, with only a door between us, keeping us apart. The perfect place to peel off every layer of clothing, taste every inch of her skin, and explore all her secret places.

I forced my eyes shut, swallowed down the unbidden groan, and turned away.

"Get dressed," I told her, shutting away all thoughts of stripping her bare and returning her to her bed, with me beside her. "We need to go."

CHAPTER 18

Kip

This had to be another one of those dreams. At any second I was going to wake up, realize that I had work in the morning and that a strange, sexy man wasn't staring at me like he wanted to bite me.

Harley had repeatedly told me over the years that I needed to buy sexier pajamas. And now, the man's eyes wouldn't stop straying down towards them. I suddenly wished I'd taken Harley up on her offer to take me to the lingerie stores in the mall. Dream me wanted to take advantage of the sexy, growley man before I woke up.

Except. My dreams usually featured me out in in public and in embarrassing underwear. While the nightshirt and shorts I was wearing weren't exactly the most elegant of ensembles, I was clothed. And this motel room certainly wasn't public. Plus, the look on Stryder's face was real.

I was awake.

I suddenly noticed the strange new face in the room.

I yelped, pointing to the blond, bearded man standing behind Stryder. "Who's that?"

"Don't worry about him for now," Stryder responded. "It's time to go."

"I want to know what's going on," I insisted, his lack of answers making me frustrated and angry. "You can't just bring some random person inside my hotel room."

"He's not a random person, he's with me."

"Everyone stop talking," Harley groaned from her bed across the room. "Or take your love spat outside."

Flipping on the light, I gestured toward Stryder and the new guy. "He brought some stranger in our room." Harley jerked up in her bed, eyes wide and blinking up at him.

"Kip, listen to me," Stryder strode over to me, his eyes drifting towards my top again. "You need to get dressed." His throat bobbed. "We need to leave, now."

"Do you know how frequently you just demand things?" I growled. Sleep-deprived Kip had made her appearance and I wasn't going to apologize for it. There was only so much this man could drag me through before the cracks started to show.

"Yes and we'll talk about it later."

"Who the hell is that?" Harley eyed the man sharply.

I gestured sharply toward Harley. "See? There's a consensus."

"Are you two twins? And why is he wearing those clothes?" Harley asked.

Stryder and his 'twin' looked at each other blankly. They looked nothing alike, except that they both had long hair and were tall and muscular. But while Stryder had dark, intense eyes and deep chestnut hair, the other guy had bright green eyes. He looked like a great, hulking Viking warrior; his hair was so light, it reminded me of soft, powdered sand on a tropical island.

He was also wearing brown trousers and a white linen shirt. They were crooked, as if he'd been in a hurry to put them on.

The blond man stepped around Stryder, but instead of

coming up to me, he walked straight over to Harley's bed. I turned, stunned, as he knelt by the side of it, holding one of her hands in his. She blinked, then turned towards me with an expression that said she was just as lost in the situation as I was.

"I am Roane, born of the Night Court, warrior of the Blood Court. It's an honor to make your acquaintance."

He touched a kiss to Harley's hand and she snatched it back like he'd bitten her. "You have got to be kidding me with that shit." She scrambled out of bed and crossed the room to me in two strides. "What is going on?"

"Fine. If this will make you dress quicker," Stryder sighed. "This is my Roane, my best friend from the Land of Sidhe. He just showed up, bringing grave news of the war. I can't wait for you to make a decision any longer, Kip. You have to come with me back to my world."

"I *have to*?" I asked incredulously. "What happened to giving me time to think this through and decide for myself?"

"There isn't time," Roane said. "The darkest time of the war is dawning. Without Stryder there, the Blood Court has no hope. And if the Blood Court falls…" His voice trailed off and his face went pale. Out of the corner of my eye, I saw Harley staring at him. Without the heavy makeup, her face held more expression and it was etched in a blend of confusion, aggravation, and allure. They were complete opposites. He was the light to her dark, in both looks and demeanor. The instant attraction to Roane was obvious, but she wasn't having any of it. It seemed to annoy her even more.

"What does that have to do with Kip?" she snapped. "Stryder is the one you need and he's right there. You came, you saw, you conquered, so go home."

Roane frowned. "I would have happily left as soon as I got here. He's the one who said we had to come for Kip."

"Oh good, so you don't care if Kip goes with you. She doesn't seem as important to your world as Stryder wants us to believe."

She folded her arms across her chest, looking at Stryder. "I'd like to say it was nice knowing you, but since you broke my car, that would be a lie."

"I did not break your car. And Roane has yet to understand the implications of her returning with us because I haven't had the time to explain it to him. As I keep trying to tell you, we're in a hurry. My kingdom is falling. I need to return to it. Now dress yourself and pack your things."

"But do I really have to go with you?" I asked.

"If Stryder stated she needed to return with us, then I'm certain it is true. He would never lie." Roane said.

"I don't know, I'm pretty sure he's told us some whoppers!" Harley spread her arms out wide. "If he were a fisherman, his fish would be this big."

I laughed, unable to stop myself.

"Kip!" I jumped at Stryder's bark. He grabbed my side and pulled me to him. His eyes stared intently into mine, his fingers digging into my skin. "Would you get some clothes on?" His voice came out strangled. "Please!"

My mouth parted at the plea, surprised. Heat pooled in my stomach at his touch, flushing up my chest and neck. I swallowed down the lump in my throat, feeling his intense gaze over every single part of my body, giving in.

"Ugh," I growled out. "Why do you always do this to me?"

"What? What's he always doing to you?" Harley asked but I ignored her as I marched over to my suitcase.

"I'll get dressed. But only because I don't like standing here in my pajamas with the two of you fully dressed. That doesn't mean I'm going with you. I still don't know what's going on or what I want to do. You're going to tell me the truth and I'll figure it out from there." Grabbing my clothes, I went to the bathroom.

"Stryder, why don't we leave her," I heard Roane's voice as I shut the door behind me. "If she needs time, give it to her. While she's considering her options, we can be fighting and bringing this war to an end. Then you can come back for her."

"It's not that simple." I heard Stryder's low growl clearly through the bathroom door. I slipped on a pair of black jeans and black T-shirt as their low, murmured voices continued.

"Look at me. I am the night," I said dramatically, stepping out of the bathroom.

Harley laughed at my super hero reference, but Stryder didn't seem impressed. Instead, his stare burned into me.

"Good. Let's go." He reached for my bag, but I stepped in between him and the bed to stop him.

"No. That wasn't the deal."

He growled and stood back up, eyes flashing.

"I know you aren't telling me the whole truth, Stryder. There's something else going on and I need to know it. This isn't asking me to hop in a car and go on a multi-state joyride with you. That was absurd enough."

"I know." His chin lifted slightly and he let out a slow breath as if trying to keep himself calm.

"You're asking me to do so much more than that now. A few days ago, I had never even seen you and now you're asking me to go to this other world and be a part of a war. I'm supposed to just accept that there is a whole place I never knew existed. That I somehow have something to do with it."

"I know the gravity of what I'm asking you to do." The words came out through teeth grit so hard, I was afraid they would all just crack and fall out.

"Do you?" I raised my eyebrow, skeptically.

"Yes!"

The word exploded out of him, making my breath catch in my throat. Stryder's intensity had risen to an extreme level. I could feel it pulsating off him in waves. I immediately wanted to comfort him. And yet, I couldn't. As drawn to him as I felt, there was also an impossible distance between us.

Roane extended a hand out to Harley. "May I assist you in packing your belongings and escort you to the nearest transportation back to your home?"

His voice was chivalrous and kind, and that seemed to throw Harley off even more.

"No."

My eyes hadn't left Stryder. "Unless you tell me everything, I can't do this. I'm not like you, Stryder. Your people, your world, your reality are complete unknowns to me. You can't just expect me to understand the importance of what's happening or what you need me to do if you don't tell me."

He drew in a breath and took a step toward me. I was pretty sure he was just going to pick me up and toss me over his back like a sack of potatoes. It was a relief when he started talking instead.

"I was not sent here for the same reason as the other men. I've already told you that. But I was sent."

"By who?"

"The wizards. My most trusted advisers. They see what others can't and know what others don't. I've counted on them to help me through this war."

"And what did they see? Did it have to do with me?"

"Yes, of course. They don't know everything and can't always say exactly what's going to happen. Even if they could, they couldn't stop it. All they can do is guide those willing to listen." He paused, and when I gave him a look to keep talking, he continued begrudgingly. "There was a prophecy. The advisers saw a woman who would change the course of the war. And that woman, is you."

I gasped. "What?"

He didn't elaborate. "The evil Summer Queen will do anything to gain the power she wants. And if that means kidnapping you, then there will be no hesitation. She will do whatever it takes to conquer us, and she will not accept a refusal on your part. She wouldn't think twice about destroying anyone who she thinks might stand in her way. That is why you need to come with me." His stare burned into me. "I can keep you safe."

I stared at him, my mind stuttering. Stryder went to the bed and shoved all the clothes I'd taken out back inside. I was cautious about all of his movements. Part of me was still bracing for the potato sack version of how this encounter would end. But he zipped my bag of clothes and held out his hand.

An invitation.

He wouldn't force me to come with him.

I wanted to ask another question, but a crash followed by the sound of splintering woods stopped it before it came out of my mouth. In its place was a scream. Roane leapt in front of Harley, pressing her back against the wall as Stryder blocked me with his body. I looked around him and saw three of the Fae men smashed the rest of their way through the door and into the room. Two were gripping something between them.

Taking a step around Stryder, I could see the men fully. My hand flew up to cover my mouth when I saw what they were dragging.

It was Mac.

CHAPTER 19

Kip

"Mac!" I screamed.

I tried to lunge toward him, but Stryder grabbed me, holding me close, not budging, even when I tried to push him away.

"Don't get near them, Kip," he warned. "It's not safe."

"Whatever would give you that impression?" one of the men asked in a voice that made a wave of disgust roll over me. "It's not like we're here to *kill* her or anything."

Even just the words coming out of his mouth sent a chill running down my spine. Stryder stiffened beside me and took a step closer, forcing me back so that his body blocked me. "Get away from her."

"What are you doing to Mac?" I shouted.

I ducked around the other side of Stryder so I didn't lose sight of Mac. He was sagging in their arms, like either his legs were too weak to hold him up or he was trying to make it harder for them to be able to maneuver him. I was hoping it was the latter. His head hung down from his shoulders at an unnatural angle. The way it lolled back and forth was unnerving. It looked like his neck wasn't fully attached anymore.

It was a relief when his head lifted and I could look directly into his face. The spark that was usually in his eyes was gone. His face was discolored and uneven, places where he had been battered obvious. Anger and protectiveness rose up in me and I wanted to rescue him. I pulled my attention away from him and to the men who were holding him.

They were Fae. I knew that. Even if Stryder hadn't told me who they were or what they were doing, I'd know they were all of his kind. I remembered the strange flickers the first time I saw the men in the bookstore. The longer I looked at them and the more I learned from Stryder, the less they seemed like flickers and the more they were shifts.

At first, looking at them showed men who were approachable and appealing. But now, I could look beyond the façade each of them presented. As it fell away, I could see them for what they really were. They were terrifying.

My gaze returned to Stryder.

It wasn't the same with him. He never flickered, never wavered from the darkly sexy, mysterious man I'd seen in the bar on the night of my birthday. I didn't know for sure what that meant, but it felt significant.

Wanting to gain my footing and sense of control in the situation, I stared at the men. I wanted them to know they weren't going to make me cower. One of them was the man who'd attacked me in the park. I didn't recognize him as having been in the bookshop, but he might have been. The others had fought Stryder just before he took Harley and me on this road trip of doom.

I wondered if Stryder'd known all along this was how it was going to end. That's why we always kept moving, didn't stop long enough to breathe, especially after I'd made the phone call to Mac.

Horror gripped me as I realized my blunder, and that Stryder had been right all along.

Mac's knees buckled and the two men holding him yanked him back up to his feet. The rough movement made him groan and a shudder of guilt rolled through me. This was my fault. If it wasn't for me, the sweet elderly man wouldn't be in this situation. He was being targeted because they had seen us together. He looked up at me and something flashed in his eyes. It was an emotion as difficult to read as it was to see.

"Mac," I called out to him, "are you all right?"

I knew he wasn't. He'd had the living hell beaten out of him. But I saw the fight behind those injuries, the fire still in his eyes. Mac hadn't just let them take him. He hadn't just gone along because he was afraid. He'd fought back.

"Can you hear the screams, Kip?" he asked.

His voice was low, but strong. At first I didn't understand the words. Then it hit me hard. His story. The tale he'd woven to entertain me over the years I'd known him wasn't a product of his imagination. It was everything Stryder had been trying to explain to me, spun into whimsical pieces for me to absorb.

"She will soon enough," one of the men said harshly. "But she'll be the one who decides who screams."

Disgust roiled through my stomach when I turned to him. "I would never."

"You come with us and then you won't have to worry about it."

"I seriously doubt that."

He scowled, taking a step closer, which brought a low growl from Stryder's voice.

"If you come with us, we'll leave him alone. Return him safe and sound."

"Don't listen to them, Kip," Mac insisted.

"It's up to you," the other man said. "You have the ability to save him. It's as simple as agreeing to come along with us. You agree to that, and we will let him go."

"We'll even bring him back to his precious bookshop before we leave. He doesn't have to go through anything else."

"Don't," Mac said. "Don't listen to them."

One of the men grabbed the back of Mac's neck and wrenched his head up so he could growl into his ear. "Maybe we should just take you apart piece by piece until she decides to save what's left."

"That's enough," Stryder said forcefully. "Leave him alone."

"Your problem is with us, not with him," Roane added. "Let him go."

"That's where you're wrong. Our issue is with Kip. But she could so easily make it all disappear." The man turned to me. "We aren't here to hurt you. We just need you to come with us. It's that simple."

I scoffed angrily. "Yes, it's that simple. Hand myself over to people who are trying to say they aren't going to hurt me, when they have kidnapped and beaten an innocent man to torment me."

"You aren't going to take her," Stryder said, his voice low and deadly.

The man tilted his head to the side. "Suddenly so protective of her. That's a change."

I looked at Stryder. "What does he mean?"

"Nothing. It doesn't matter now."

"Doesn't matter?" the Fae man laughed, his voice changing now as he realized he had gotten his claws into Stryder. "I guess that means you haven't told her the truth about why you're here. Why you are the last person she is safe with."

"This isn't about me."

"Of course it is. The whole war is about you. If you would only submit to Queen Ajeka and her rule, the war would be over, and Kip wouldn't be needed. She deserves to know why you came for her, Stryder. Don't you think she should know what she is really facing?"

CHAPTER 20

Stryder

"Stop, Xavier," I commanded.

It couldn't be like this. Kip couldn't find out this way. She deserved more than that.

"Why?" Xavier asked in the taunting voice that made me want to pummel him until he couldn't speak another word. "It really looks like the two of you have gotten very cozy since you got here. It seems to me she should understand who she is putting her trust in before she decides where she is really safe."

I lunged for Xavier, but he pulled back, his arm pressed against Mac's throat. The older man's eyes met mine and the expression in them forced me to take a step back. It had been so long since I'd seen him. When I first walked into the bookshop to talk to Kip and saw Mackenzie, I thought my mind might be playing tricks on me. But he knew who I was the instant our eyes locked. His face was lined and weathered, but the laughter in his blue eyes was the exact same as it had been when I was young and said goodbye to him the last time.

Mackenzie"s disappearance from the Land of Sidhe had haunted many of us. A powerful man, he had worked to guard the Blood Court and protect the records of our people. He knew things no one else did and it was that knowledge that made him a target. When he disappeared, everyone feared he had finally found himself on the wrong end of a sword. I could still remember the devastation on my parents' faces in the weeks that followed as teams searched, only to come to the conclusion he was gone.

Seeing him again was at once thrilling and horrifying. He knew so much and that only made the danger sharper.

"I want to know what they're talking about," Kip commanded. "Stryder, tell me."

"I've told you about the prophecy. You are meant to be an important part of the war. The Summer Queen will continue to destroy the Courts and the land. Continue to destroy lives. Those opposed to her will push back against her. She will face opposition that will threaten her rule and her life."

"Tell her the rest," Xavier taunted me.

"Stryder." Kip sounded angry, and I knew I couldn't keep it from her any long. "I am fighting to stop the Queen, but the prophecy about you. You weren't going to stop her. You were going to save her." Kip looked shocked, startled by what I was telling her. She took a step back as if the words themselves had shoved her.

"These men came to bring me to the queen and make sure I save her," she said as the realization sank in. "But you…"

"I was sent to stop you."

"Such a gentle way of saying you were sent to kill her," Keilen snapped.

"Shut up, Keilen."

Kip's mouth fell open. Her eyes burned into me, the betrayal in them searing my skin. "Tell me they're lying."

I wanted to. More than anything, I wanted to preserve the trust she had in me. But I couldn't. There was nothing I could say or do. That had all been shattered and all that was left now was stopping her from falling into their control.

"I won't hurt you," I told her. "Not now. I know you. You would never help the Queen.'"

"Not now?" She shook her head, her pain betrayed by the squeak in her voice. "How comforting."

I held my hand to her. "Kip."

She shook her head, backing away from me.

"You don't have to trust him," Xavier said. "Come with us. Let us bring you to our queen. You only know what Stryder has told you. Do you really think he would tell you the truth? A man sent here to kill you? Let us bring you to her so you can understand her for yourself. You'll see that she is not the one who needs to be stopped. Mac will live and you will be protected. His life rests in your hands."

"Don't let them manipulate you," Roane said. "Look at what they're doing. They won't protect you for a second longer than you're needed to save the queen. If you go with them, the lives of everyone in the Fae realm are at risk."

Kip's eyes flashed back and forth between me and the Fae men holding Mac. The third Fae stood close to Roane and Harley, they were bracing for an attack. I knew there was no simple way to get out of this. I had to get them to release Mac and leave Kip alone. It was the only way.

I attacked Xavier first, by tackling him into a table, sending it into a splintering mess. The impact forced him to let go of Mac as I flattened him into the furniture. The cheap wood shattered on the ground near us, and the television bolted onto the wall fell off one of its hinges, hanging sideways. Xavier's fists pounded into my back as he tried to get me off of him, but I threw my own into his ribs, hearing the sound of several breaking. I knew Keilen was going to pull me off soon, and I had to deal as much damage as possible as quickly as possible. When Keilen yanked me back, Xavier's punches had weakened and slowed.

Keilen was now on top of me and we rolled, the bed stopping the movement. I smashed his head into the metal frame of it and wrapped my arm around his neck in a chokehold, sliding to the side so I could be behind him. One arm flailed at me and I caught it, hooking it behind him and wrenching upward to add pressure on his shoulder while choking him out. He screamed a list of labored obscenities and slowly began going limp. Just as he was about to go out, I wrenched as hard as I could on his elbow, pulling up on his arm until I heard an audible snap in his shoulder.

Roane was holding Harley and Kip back, who was struggling against him. "You need to get to safety," he yelled at them.

I rolled out from Keilen and turned to see the third man, one I didn't immediately recognize, hovering over Mac. His arm was back like he was going to punch him, and he was turned away from me. Jumping to my feet, I grabbed his arm and thrust forward, knocking him temporarily off balance. As soon as he lost his footing, I shifted weight and brought his arm down. He flipped over my body and crashed to the floor. He raised his head and a stunned expression on his face matched the garbled sound that raged from his throat. I didn't let him finish the thought before I stomped his head into the ground, knocking him unconscious.

Spinning back to Mackenzie, I looked him over to check for major injuries. Before I could get much of an assessment, Xavier yanked me off my feet. We crashed into the wall opposite. He must have had a little left in the tank, as he rained down punches on my head. I put my arms up to defend myself. Curling in, I created a ball with my body and then exploded outward, kicking my feet and using the momentum to kick up into a standing position. Xavier stumbled backward and I pounced, shoving my knee into his throat and forcing him to the ground. As my fists hammered down on his face and he slowly stopped responding, I could hear Harley screaming at Kip. Looking up, I could see Kip tearing away from Roane and running out of the hotel room.

CHAPTER 21

Kip

I had to run. There was no other choice. With any luck, they would leave Mac on the grungy industrial carpet and chase after me. Of course, I might not get away from them. But that wasn't going to stop me. Even if I was just running to put distance between myself and the hotel, to act as bait to pull them away from the old man I considered a part of my family, that was enough. At least then I would only be responsible for my own safety. If they caught me, I was the only one in danger.

The walls were closing in on me. There was a part of me that was running just to get out of that space. What the men told me about Stryder pressed down on my shoulders and swirled in my mind. I didn't know what to think. The beginnings of trust had started and now they were blown to bits. I had no idea what to think or who I should trust. Everything seemed like a lie and my brain couldn't decide where to land.

Running let me think about nothing but my feet on the ground.

The sun beat down on me as I ran through the blistering

daylight. If the sun was down, I could disappear into the shadows and make it harder for the men to follow me. Even though I knew they could track me, the darkness would at least let me stay slightly ahead. Every second mattered.

I had only been running for a few seconds before I heard them coming after me. I pushed as hard as I could into the sprawling field beside the hotel. There was something ahead, dark shapes against the horizon, and I was headed for them. Behind me voices, shouting and snarling at each other, told me everyone from the hotel room was coming close behind. I glanced behind my shoulder enough to see a Fae man dragging Mac.

I stumbled, frustrated that they were still dragging Mac with them.

"Run," Mac shouted.

His words made my feet spurt forward again and finally, my feet brought me to the edge of the field. I ducked through a broken part in an old chain link fence. The lot around me looked like it had once belonged to a fabricating business or construction company. Twisted metal, piles of lumber and other materials, and discarded equipment cluttered the dirt patch. They created a congested, terrifying maze. It was exactly what I needed.

I dove behind the carcass of an old car. Seconds later I saw Xavier and Keilen drag Mac into the open space a few yards in front of me. Shouts in the distance told me the others were in a scuffle somewhere in the field. It was just the four of us now.

"Come out, Kip," Xavier commanded. "You don't have to make this so difficult."

"No," Mac shouted. "Go. Get away."

Keilen smashed the back of his head with his fist, making Mac sag.

"Go get her," Xavier told the other Fae man.

Keilen released Mac and started toward me, twisting at his injured shoulder.

Suddenly Mac threw his body into Xavier, smashing his head into his nose, and sent a stream of blood flying. Finally being loose from his grip, he took off, scrambling for the cover of a broken-down car. Before he could reach it, Keilen dove at his feet, tripping him and causing him to land hard on the ground. Mac turned, thrusting one hand out, and Keilen looked up in horror.

A whirring sound filled the air around them, and a bright white light grew around Mac's hand. It was as if one of those old-timey light bulbs was in his palm, the type that take a moment to warm up, but then produce an almost impossible amount of light. The sound built for just a moment and then erupted into a sonic scream, and Keilen was washed in that white light. His features disappeared and I couldn't make out if he had screamed over the piercing sound. I covered my ears and fell to my knees to fight it.

Then, with a little click and a hiss, like the sound of a soda can being opened, the sonic scream was gone. Keilen was unconscious, his hand limp on Mac's leg. I looked from his hand to Mac's face and he met my gaze.

"Run, damn it," he screamed at me.

But I couldn't move. My legs were rooted to the spot. My mind, blank in shock.

Mac, my Mac, was one of *them*.

Betrayal and horror washed over me. My Mac. How could he? I trusted him for *years*, he was like a second father to me, and now, he isn't who I thought he was.

Mac was standing now, pain etched on his face with every step. He reached his hand for me, as if he could read my thoughts. As if he could wash away the betrayal I was feeling inside. But he was running toward me, and in what seemed like the blink of an eye he was tackling me behind a rusted-out metal bin. Sparks and fire shot over the top of it from Xavier, who had recovered and was using some kind of projectile magic to fire at us. Mac sat up and looked at me, his eyes imploring. When he spoke, it was low, authoritative, but mired in desperation.

"I'm sorry, Kip. I didn't mean for it to end like this."

"*End?*" My voice was incredulous. "What do you mean, end?"

"Run, Kip. Run until you are safe. And don't listen to them, no matter what they say. Run, I'll distract them. Now, go!"

Jumping to his feet, Mac dove from behind the bin and rolled, finding himself behind a pillar. He faked a step forward and a blast of magic nearly took him out, but he managed to stop his momentum first. Then he ran again, diving behind what at one time had been a wall. "Kip! Run!"

A feeling like a bubble bursting inside my head happened, and I was filled with an instant sense of focus. If I didn't run now, we both might end up dead. I had to go. Now.

My feet started moving before I knew where to go, and I realized I was running in the direction of the woods. I chanced a look behind me and saw Mac firing a bolt of whatever magic he had left at Xavier, who deftly avoided it, and then fired back. The wall crumbled, and I could hear a mangled cry. Mac was fighting with everything he had in him and I was terrified it wouldn't be enough.

No, I couldn't leave him like this. I turned around, determined to help him. I wouldn't let them kill him.

I ran back down the hill and through the trees. I could just make out the shard of a small building that Mac had hidden behind. A gnarled piece of metal swung up from it, Mac's final bid for survival. I screamed his name, fear gripping me as it was met with a blast of magic. Bits of metal and billows of red misted the air. I stared in shock, still running towards him. "Mac! Mac!"

When the dust died down, there was no more movement.

The Fae stood over it and reached down into the rubble. He yanked at the lifeless body of Mac and then dropped him, spinning around to look for me. Looking in multiple directions, his eyes finally found me. I shrunk under his gaze, skidding to a stop, as his lips twisted up in a triumphant smile.

Tears streaming down my face, I doubled back around. I put my head down and ran as fast as I could, finding a hill and darting up it and into a line of trees. Sobbing, grief pounding my chest, I ran blindly until my body smashed into something and arms encircled me. Screaming, I thrashed against the grip.

"Kip, stop it."

Stryder's voice broke through the terror. I looked up at him and he stared down into my eyes. Behind him, Roane held the third Fae man to the ground.

"They killed him," I sobbed. "They killed Mac."

A growl formed low in Stryder's chest and rose up his throat until it poured out of his mouth in a roar. Putting me down, he took off across the field, Roane abandoning the third man to chase after him. I should have turned in the other direction and escaped, but I couldn't bring myself to do it. I had just watched them destroy one of the most important people in my life and I couldn't just leave. Harley shouted after me as I ran after them, but I refused to even turn around. Soon she was running along beside me.

We burst back into the cluttered industrial yard and Xavier and Keilen rushed toward us.

"Gray, get her!" Xavier shouted.

I heard it just in time to weave out of the way and run into the tangle of abandoned equipment and metal. The man followed me so close I could feel his breath on the back of my neck.

"Get away from her!" Stryder shouted.

The man shot backwards as if grabbed by some unseen force and was tossed several yards away. I ran only a few more feet before finding Harley. She'd come around the other side and caught me, grabbing me and starting to pull me back toward the field.

"We have to get Mac," I told her. "I can't leave him."

"We have to get out of here," Harley said. "Stryder is pissed and this is about to get ugly."

CHAPTER 22

Stryder

A blast of magic exploded into a crane beside me and I spun to look at where it had come from. Ducking behind debris of their own were Keilen, Xavier and Gray. I turned back to Kip, but Harley was already dragging her away. Roane was tugging at my arm to get me to do the same. I shook him off and charged the three Fae men instead, and behind me I heard Roane mutter a curse and take off after me.

Gray tried to duck his head out to see where I had gone, but I was already on top of him. I tackled him to the ground as Roane sent a blast of magic toward Keilen and Xavier. They ducked and scrambled out of the way as limbs of the trees crashed around them, and Roane ducked down behind a large boulder. I was busy laying punches into the midsection of Gray as he attempted to kick me off. I held on to his jacket and yanked him face-first into the boulder Roane was hiding behind. A smattering of blood smeared the rock and I saw him losing consciousness.

Roane jumped to his feet and fired again, then ducked back

down behind me. I grabbed Gray's head and was smashing it into the rock now, over and over, a scream welling up in my chest and seeming to burst forth out of every pore. Finally, I felt a hand on my shoulder, and I spun to look at Roane, his battle-hardened face grimacing in a recognition of yet another horror of war.

"He's dead, Stryder. Help me now," he said, and I looked back to the head in my hands.

It was mangled, blood covering my hands and running in trickles into the leaves below. The rock was dripping with it, and with pieces of the inside of his head, where his skull was cracked like a coconut. I let it drop from my hands, and it landed with the grace of a sandbag being thrown. Gray was no more, and now there were only two.

I looked back to Roane, who was watching the others with the intensity and focus that gave away his years of experience. His eyes flicked to me and back to them before he muttered under his breath, "They are splitting up, one heading back toward the field and the other moving right, away from him. They want us to split up. I think they think Gray is still in this, and he can pull up the rear. Go get Keilen, and I'll keep Xavier busy."

"No," I said, shaking my head.

Anger was filling every inch of me now and was going to fuel everything that happened for the next few moments. It was useful in that way, for a soldier at least. Anger—true, blood-boiling anger—made you focus. It made you think of the worst possible things to do to someone, and then how to get them done. Xavier had killed Mac, and because of it, he was going to suffer at my hands.

"What do you want to do?"

"I want to kill Xavier. Do what you want with Keilen," I said.

Roane looked at me expressionless for a moment. His mouth

pursed like he was making a decision and then he opened it again. "Do you want him alive?"

"I said do what you want."

His mouth closed again, and the faintest hint of a grin stretched it. He nodded and trooped off, searching for his prey. I knew what he wanted, and it was the same as me. He wanted revenge, and he was going to get it. As he went off, I stood, not charging a magical blast, not hiding behind anything, just standing in the open.

There was a moment of silence, only punctuated by the sound of Roane's boots crossing the forest away from us.

"Come out, Xavier. You and me, now," I said. More silence greeted me, and I made my voice louder. In the distance, I could hear a shifting and knew Harley and Kip were hiding in a cluster of downed trees. "Come out, Xavier. Fight me."

In the distance, a shadow stood up against the setting sun. It unfurled itself and squared toward me. It paused a moment, and then stepped over a fallen branch as if waiting for me to fire at him. When I didn't, it emboldened him and he began to walk closer, more confidently. When he got within a few steps, his face fell from the shadows and he grinned.

"I look forward to finally ending yo—" Xavier began, but before he could muster any other words, I had rushed forward, planting my fist into his jaw.

In the distance I heard the sound of swords clashing. The reverberation of their blades through the afternoon stillness told me Roane and Keilen had returned to the weapons we were most comfortable with using. I left mine where it was. My anger and protectiveness for Kip were primal, and that's exactly how I wanted this fight. Xavier would meet his end not at the edge of my blade, but by my hands.

He reeled backward, a sound of surprise fumbling from his lips as he struggled to get his feet under him. I jumped at him, kicking him in the stomach and sending him farther back and into the ground on his belly. He tried to flip onto his back, but I was on top of him already, raining down punches into his eyes, feeling the bones crunch under my fist and skin tear away, blood escaping into the freedom of the outside.

Xavier tried to punch back, but I grabbed his arm under my own and shifted my knee into his elbow. I broke it, sending him howling in pain. His useless arm dangled as he tried to scramble away from me, but my weight held him down. I smashed my elbow into his jaw. After a few of those, his body began to go limp. I stopped, flipping him over and shaking him until his glazed eyes tried to focus on me. I leaned down, just inches from his nose and shook him again until I knew I had his attention.

"You killed Mac. You threatened Kip," I spat at him, and his brows furrowed, but he was too weak to respond. "Now you will pay for it."

I raised one hand and called from deep within me the magic that I knew was forbidden outside of war. The energy filled my hand, and the sonic sound whirred around us. Xavier looked at my hand and then into my eyes and his grew round and wide. My magic was stronger than most, and this spell, one that would simply disable from most Fae, was a killing blow in my hands.

I wanted more than his death. I wanted his pain.

I pushed my hand down into his chest, and felt the burning sensation go through me and into his heart. The magic pulled at my energy, but I held strong, pushing into the exhaustion and allowing it to consume me in my effort. I knew that inside of Xavier, his entire body was on fire from the inside out. An intense pain unlike any other was consuming him, and every millisecond he lived with it was an eternity.

I held it there for a long time, unwilling to deal the killing blow. He had to suffer. To feel the pain of the loss I felt for Mac.

His eyes were wide and frozen on me, I could see the torture in them and I reveled in it.

Then I noticed a sound beside me. Kip was running toward us, Harley right behind her, trying to pull her back. She looked down at Xavier. Her face turned to a grimace and she nodded at me. I sent a powerful blast from my hand and then released the spell. His body went limp and smoke came from behind his eyes and out of his mouth where his insides had turned to ashes.

I slumped off of him and looked into the distance, where another shadow was walking toward me against the sun. It was Roane. He walked up to me and looked down at the body of Xavier, a moment of shock crossing his face before he looked back at me.

"The burning heart?" he asked, his eyes wide and searching mine.

With what I was going through, it was only appropriate.

"Yes," I managed, my body struggling to regain the energy it had taken out of me.

Roane looked back at the dead body of Xavier and then spat.

"Good," he said, and then held his hand out.

I took it and we stood, Harley and Kip joining us. The redness of her eyes made my chest ache even as I celebrated the victory.

"Why are you smiling?" she asked. "Mac is dead and it's my fault."

"It isn't your fault."

"Yes, it is. If it wasn't for me, none of this would have happened. I failed him." She looked in the direction of the pile of rubble where his body still lay. "He's one of you, isn't he?" I could hear the ache of betrayal in her voice.

"Yes. I haven't seen him in many years. He disappeared from the Fae realm when I was still young. No one had been able to find him."

"And I just conveniently started working for him not knowing this prophecy was hanging over my head."

"You can't think that way," Roane told her. "None of us know why you were chosen. Mac being a part of your life may have had nothing to do with it."

"And it may have."

The pain in her voice was heart-wrenching and worse was the knowledge that she was right. It wasn't a coincidence that she'd ended up working for a Fae. Something had brought her to that bookshop.

"But those men are dead now," Harley said encouragingly. "You can feel safe again. We can go home and go back to our lives."

"No," I told her, shaking my head.

Roane stepped up close to Harley. The pull between them was obvious, even if both were doing their best to dig in their heels and resist the attraction.

"What do you mean?"

"They weren't all of them. The queen has many more followers. She will send as many as it takes to bring Kip to her."

"It isn't just that," I said. "Ajeka will send more to try to kidnap Kip, but they are only one danger. Soon the wizards will know I didn't complete my mission. It won't change their intention."

"You mean they will send someone else to try to kill me."

I nodded solemnly. "Yes. Unless you come with me, and I will convince them otherwise."

"Well, isn't that fabulous. I literally can't win. No matter what corner I turn, someone is going to be there to either try to kidnap me or kill me. I'll never be safe."

"Maybe not now, but you can be," I said. "Come back with Roane and me."

"Go where there are even more people who want me dead or to use me as a queen insurance policy?"

"Go back and fight with us. We don't know what it is about you that is so powerful that you are meant to protect the queen. But the very thing that has the power to give and protect life has the power to destroy it. Instead of guarding her and ensuring victory for her side, you could help us bring her down."

CHAPTER 23

Kip

I didn't really know Mac.

That was what was sinking in in those moments while Stryder and Roane were trying to convince me of all the reasons I should go back to their world. I had spent so much time with the eccentric, kind, brilliant man. And yet I had never really known him.

As much as I wanted to believe there might be no link between me working in Mac's shop and the prophecy that was designed to draw me into their world, I knew that couldn't be the case.

All along, I thought I knew him, that he looked after me because of the time we'd spent getting to know each other. Because of the bond that we'd formed. And now, I doubted everything.

And yet, his death cut though me like a razor-sharp sword.

I was overwhelmed by sadness at the loss of my friend, moved by his willingness to give up his life to protect mine.

I wouldn't let it be in vain. If there was something I could do, anything, to avenge Mac and prevent more imminent deaths of innocent people, it was what had to be done. My fear didn't matter anymore. It didn't even matter that I still didn't fully understand what was happening or why. This was at my feet now, my responsibility to take it up and carry it as far as I needed to.

I turned to Stryder, my heart aching.

I was more wary of him than I had been when I first saw him, and that wariness sent pain shooting through me. Knowing he was protecting me was what had carried me through. Now I knew it wasn't a desire to keep me safe that had brought him to Glendale. He had been sent to kill me. My mind went back to the day at the park and the dagger clutched in his hand. It had been so easy then to believe he was holding it to protect me from the man coming up behind me. I never questioned why he had it with him in the first place.

That resistance couldn't stop me. He might have come to my world to kill me, but he hadn't done it. I was still alive and as long as that was true, I would do whatever could be done to end the innocent bloodshed.

"What's going to happen to Mac's body? We can't just leave it there."

"We will make sure he is sent back to the Fae realm. It's the least we can do for his sacrifice."

The word hung heavily in the air and for a few seconds my mind drifted away to somewhere else, to what my reality might be if Stryder had never walked into that bar. If none of them had ever come for me.

"I'll go with you."

My words cut Stryder off in the middle of a sentence and he looked like he wasn't sure he'd actually heard me correctly.

"You will?" he asked.

"Isn't that what you want?"

He nodded, looking over at Roane and then back at me.

"Yes, of course. I just didn't expect you to agree so quickly. You've been, how should I say it, less than compliant throughout this experience. I honestly expected to have to do more convincing."

"And possibly just grab you and bring you with us," Roane added.

"Because threats of kidnapping are always the way to a girl's heart," Harley said snidely.

"Her heart is not my concern right now."

The emphasis on *her* wasn't lost on me, or on Harley. She looked away, and if I didn't know any better, I'd think a bit of color splashed across her cheeks for only a second.

I stared the guys down. "This isn't for you. I'm not agreeing to go because either of you asked me to. Neither of you have exactly been able to make the most compelling of arguments for me to want to just jump on your bandwagon. And, frankly, traveling with someone I know planned at least one, and possibly several, ways to kill me is not my idea of the ideal first entry in my travel blog."

"Kip, I will never hurt you," Stryder stepped towards me, intensity and anguish in his gaze.

I held up a hand to stop him. "That isn't what I'm thinking about right now. I'm thinking about Mac and what happened to him. If those men are her followers and could kill him so easily, I know the queen isn't one to be underestimated." I looked into his eyes, shoring up my courage and determination. "But neither am I."

A grin broke out on his face and for a moment there was no one else in the world but him and me. I was caught up in his gaze, the way he looked at me, with a deep, intense *need*. I forced myself to look away, to break the connection between us. Stryder was not my friend. I was here to help his people, and then move on with my life.

Stryder took a step back, then looked at Roane. "We'll get

back and confer with the wizards. They'll help us decide what to do next. Let's get back to the hotel and get you ready."

"I'm going too," Harley said. She strolled right past them and into the field, headed back to the hotel.

The men were no longer amused. "You can't come with us," Stryder said, starting after her.

"Not really your choice."

"Actually, it is absolutely my choice."

"You wish."

"The war is no place for you," Roane said to her, his voice full of concern and ineffectually veiled tenderness.

"Who are you to decide what is a place for me and what isn't?"

"You are not a part of this," he said. "This doesn't involve you. Besides, we can't take you away from the world you know and everything that matters to you. Especially for something so dangerous."

"I'd like to point out that both of you are very willingly, and almost forcibly, but I admit without mal-intent, taking Kip with you. She might be agreeing to go now, but you said yourself you would have just scooped her up and brought her with you if she didn't agree. And she is nowhere near as equipped as I am to handle dangerous people and things."

"Kip is a different situation," Stryder pointed out. "She is fated to be there, to be a part of the war, and to be with me. She is meant to be there and that supersedes anything that might be here."

His eyes flashed over to me as if he was gauging my reaction to what he said. Some of his words stood out more strongly than others. *And to be with me.* I didn't know what he meant but hearing him say it made my throat feel tight and painful with emotion.

I was thankful for Harley's voice when it broke through the tension.

"I don't have any real links keeping me in Glendale. I was never adopted. I have no family, no partner, no important friends other than Kip, and making this list is fucking depressing, so I'm just going to conclude with... I'm coming."

"You aren't coming," Stryder told her as we all continued to move across the field. "We don't need someone else to watch over while we're dealing with all this."

"Look, you're not going to have to watch over me. I can handle myself." She stopped, turning around to stare at him with her hands on her hips. "Besides, I'm not just going to let you take Kip. You talk about refusing to bring me away from the world I know and everything I have. Well, Kip is what I have. And I am what she has. You're not going to just take her somewhere alone."

Stryder let out a sigh of exasperation. "Fine," he said. "You can come, but don't expect us to go out of our way to protect you if you get yourself in trouble."

"I'd never dream of it." She grinned.

I walked back into the destroyed hotel room in a daze. Somewhere in my mind I was fully aware that this was my choice, yet it didn't quite feel real. Without saying anything, I walked into the bathroom and stood under the hot shower until the sound of Stryder pounding on the door brought me out.

CHAPTER 24

Stryder

Kip paced back and forth across the hotel room a few times, opening and closing the dresser drawers even though they were empty. Finally, she stopped at the end of the bed and stared at her bag. It was still sitting where I'd left it when trying to pack everything before the other Fae arrived. She stood staring at it silently until I stepped up beside her and rested a hand on her back.

"Are you okay?" I asked.

She shifted away from my touch and reached out to fold a few of the articles of clothing, like she just needed something to do with her hands.

"No. But I think that's to be expected. This is all kind of a lot."

"I know it is. Is there anything I can do to make it easier for you?"

"No. It was my decision to go with you. I'm just going to throw myself into it and try not to think about anything else. That's the only way I can imagine getting through this. There's really nothing else I can do now. I made my choice and I'm committed to it now."

"That would be a lot more compelling if you stopped talking," Harley said.

I knew what she meant. Kip kept saying the same things over and over, just with creative jumbling of words and rearrangement of the sentences.

Obviously, she was still uncertain about leaving.

As long as she was still talking, there was no need to get her stuff together or leave the hotel again. She was convinced talking was going to somehow change the progression of time. Nothing could happen, no other steps could be taken, as long as she didn't move on from what she was saying.

But that's not how it worked. The more she babbled, the longer we would be delayed in the hotel and the more likely it was another wave of the Summer Queen's minions would come for us. We needed to go.

"What's the weather like in your world?"

I stared at Kip, thrown off by the strange question. "The weather?"

"Did you run out of things to say and have reverted to small talk?" Harley asked.

"Give me a little more credit than that," Kip snapped. "I've never been to this place and have no idea what to expect. I want to make sure I pack the right things for the weather. Nothing's worse than showing up somewhere and having nothing but a bathing suit when it's sixty degrees and storming, so you have to buy an exorbitantly expensive sweatshirt, or expecting to need that sweatshirt some other time and it ends up being stuffy and hot. I just want to be prepared."

She was starting to drift again, but at least I could follow it.

"You probably shouldn't worry about bringing too many clothes with you."

"I don't think I like the sound of that," she said.

"I only mean you'll probably want clothing and other things that fit in with the realm. There aren't only just Fae there and it will be easier for you to blend in with the others if you dress the part."

She nodded and turned to Harley.

"Just pack everything up and we'll put it in the car," Harley said, taking charge. "We can leave it in the trunk."

Several more long minutes stretched on before everything had been loaded into the trunk of the car. I chose not to point out that this wasn't Harley's car, but the one she had, as she put it, 'borrowed' from the mechanic's parking lot. That meant that if the police were able to track down the vehicle, they'd find all of Harley's and Kip's belongings stuffed into the trunk.

"Where's the portal?" Kip asked.

"Not far from here. It'll be faster if we drive."

We all piled into the car and I drove in tense silence. Despite having killed the three servants of the Summer Queen, I still expected more to appear out of nowhere and block our way. My only comfort came from Kip's powerful determination. I'd seen the fire in her eyes, the conviction in the set of her mouth, her need to avenge Mackenzie's death.

She would do whatever it took to ensure we got to my world. Once there, we could send for Mac's body and ensure he was honored.

Just as I expected, the drive to the portal took less than half an hour. This was one I hadn't used before but I knew of its location. Purposely parking the car several yards away from the portal, I stepped out and the others gathered around me. Kip and Harley stayed close together, and I noticed Harley inching slightly closer to Roane. They still clashed when they spoke, but she seemed far more willing to listen to him than to me. That was fine. If he could keep her in line, it was less complication for me.

"Moving through the portals is fast, but it isn't necessarily easy," I told the two women. "You need to hold on tightly, so you don't fall off and get lost in the portal."

"Well, that's ominous," Kip said.

"Just hang on tight and you'll be fine."

The portal was located on the side of a rocky hill. We climbed the narrow dirt path until we reached the gap between two boulders. Markings on the stone that would look to anyone else like amateurish graffiti. But I knew them as the marks of the wizards who had created the portals long ago.

I looked to Roane. "Are you ready?"

"Absolutely."

He reached down and took Harley's hand at the same time I interlaced my fingers with Kip's. She tensed under my touch, but I held her firmly. If she shook free of me during the passage through the portal, she could be lost and never found. Roane and I reached forward and clamped our hands down on each other's shoulders. Stepping to the side, we wedged ourselves into the gap between the rocks. Ensuring we each touched some of the carvings, we spoke the words to activate the portal.

Seconds later, there was a feeling like being sucked through a narrow tunnel. It felt like a harsh blast of air was forcing us through one end, while a vacuum sucked us from the other. Kip's hand started to loosen in mine, and I held her even more tightly. Roane and I had traveled through portals countless times before and knew how to maintain our position exactly to maintain our direction. Holding onto each other and to the women helped to balance us and keep the new travelers safe.

Finally, the end of the portal came, and we arrived in a clearing. Roane and I released each other and checked the women. Both seemed slightly stunned by the experience, but in one piece.

As soon as she had her bearings, Kip gasped as she looked around, taking it all in. "It's beautiful," she whispered. "Just like Mac said it would be."

The words were no more out of her mouth when I noticed her eyes discover the tendrils of black smoke twisting and convulsing across the sky in the distance. She drew in a breath and I knew her lungs had filled with the damp, acrid smells of war. She started to take a step, then looked down and noticed the trickle of blood like a tiny creek meandering at her feet.

There was a crackling noise and we looked up to see a group of bogles crowded around a fire. These were the most wicked kind of the Goblins, and they liked to stake out the portals, ready to attack anyone coming through.

The body of a large animal, hacked into pieces, was cooking over the fire pit. The body of a dead, male Fae lay next to the largest bogle, with parts of his body missing. My stomach churned as I realized it might not be an animal over the fire.

The large bogle's head snapped towards us and he stumbled to his feet, his eyes narrowed on Kip and Harley. "Well don't you look delicious."

Five other heads twisted towards us at the same time, as the large bogle drew his knife and grinned, showing his razor-sharp teeth dripping with venom. I swallowed down bile when I noticed the piece of flesh stuck in between two teeth.

The bogles lived in the forest, and stole, raped and had a taste for fat, especially delicate feminine flesh. There was no time to hesitate, no time to ease Kip into her new surroundings.

Grabbing Kip, I called out for my horse, Ominous Thunder, knowing he wouldn't be far. It took only moments for Thunder to come galloping toward me. The sheen of his black coat was like a pool of oil and his back was broad and strong. He had seen so much with me and I considered him as much a warrior as the other Fae under my command.

"Welcome to the Land of Sidhe," I murmured as I wrapped my arm around Kip's waist and swept her up with me onto the animal's back. Eyes wide on the bogles now running towards us, she crushed her body back into me. I pressed my hand to her stomach protectively, holding her tight, as a slight clenching of my thighs had Thunder bolting towards the trees.

Her petite body against mine felt so warm and comforting against my chest.

So right.

The sounds of the bogle's cries rang through the forest indicated that they were close behind us. Bogles were fast as lightening. Suddenly, there was a sharp prickling on my leg and a brush of wind as the large Bogle passed, cutting me with his poisoned knife. And then he appeared before us, with his five other men, armed to the teeth, and ready to fight.

I growled out, my protective instincts for Kip raging through me as I gripped her tighter.

I would do whatever it took to keep her safe, and kill any man or fae who stood in my path. I pulled out my sword and unfurled my wings from their bindings, spreading them out in all their glory like an angel of war. It was time to fight.

Made in the USA
Lexington, KY
27 July 2019